REVVED UP

SONOMA SERIES BOOK 4

MAE HARDEN

For my husband, who supports me every single day and laughs when I ask him to wear the gray sweatpants.

Everything good in my life is because of him.

1

PARKER

I like bad boys. At least, I like them *in theory*. Growing up the chunky, glasses wearing daughter of a pastor and a librarian, my experience with boys was limited to supervised dates with the closeted son of the assistant pastor. He was as much a bad boy as he was into me, which is to say, not at all.

But a girl can fantasize. And when I do, it's about a tall, long haired, tattoo-covered, dark and handsome someone on a motorcycle. He steals me away on the back of his Hog, the engine rumbling between my thighs as we fly down the road, wind whipping through my hair—

"PARKER!"

I yelp and tumble backwards off my stool, landing hard on the wood floor.

"Oh my God, I'm so sorry!" Lilah exclaims as she rushes around the counter to help me.

"Ow," I moan, rubbing the back of my head as I sit up.

"Jesus, you're as clumsy as me," Lilah holds out a hand to help me up.

I take it, pulling myself to my feet and brushing myself off. Not that the floors are dirty. I'm meticulous about keeping my little book-shop clean.

"You ok?" my friend asks with an apologetic grimace.

"Oh, I'm fine. Just a little bruise. You scared me!"

Lilah laughs, her green eyes full of mischief. "I called your name like three times! You were super spaced out.... What were you thinkin' about?" She wiggles her eyebrows at me, and I'm sure I blush.

She picks up the book I dropped on the counter, eyeing the cover. A shirtless man, all bulging muscles and long windswept hair graces the cover. A model-gorgeous woman sits behind him on a motorcycle, her arms draped all over him while he glowers into the distance. *Le sigh*.

"Didn't you finish this already?" she asks. "Book club is in two and a half hours.".

"I finished it! I've read it twice already. I was just flipping through it again before book club."

"Well, that explains the thousand-yard stare," Lilah laughs as she sets the book back on the counter. "God, this one was hot. You have good taste, and that's coming from someone who isn't even into the whole rugged-motorcycle-man thing."

She sets a bag on the counter next to my vintage typewriter. It doesn't work, but it looks so good in the shop that I can't part with it. I peek inside the brown paper bag.

"Seltzer?" I ask her with a little frown.

"And wine. Don't get your panties in a twist, Parker." She winks as she unloads the party supplies for tonight. "I got carried away with the Cabernet last weekend. I need a booze free night tonight."

Pfft. Yeah, right. More like she's pregnant and not telling anyone yet. We've only been friends a couple of months, but there's no way the Lilah I know is voluntarily giving up a glass of red wine.

"Okay," I say noncommittally as I try to keep my eyebrow from creeping up my face. I snag the little brown box stamped with the Olive Branch Bakery logo and crack the top, taking a deep breath of chocolate infused air. A small moan escapes my lips.

Lilah laughs. "Don't get too excited. We're experimenting with new flavors and we need guinea pigs. There are some weird ones in there."

"I volunteer as tribute," I sigh, resisting the temptation to steal one of the shiny little truffles before the others arrive. I close the box and set it aside for later.

"You say that now but wait until you hit the rosemary caramel. It's... different." Lilah grins and hands me a salad in a takeout container with big toasty pieces of ciabatta on the side. "I know you don't have time to eat dinner between closing and book club."

"God, I love you," I say, taking the salad and giving her a one-armed hug.

"Love you too, girl!" Lilah returns my hug and fixes my hair, pulling it over one shoulder. "Can I steal your hair? I just want to be a redhead for a day," she sighs. I think she's crazy. Her shiny dark hair and oversized emerald eyes make her look like a Disney princess. Ok, a very foul-mouthed version of a Disney princess.

"Sure, but good luck taming my curls," I laugh as she kisses me on the cheek.

"Deal! I'll see you tonight." Lilah hugs me fiercely before heading back to the bakery. She practically floats out of the store.

I lean on the counter and look out on my quiet store, contemplating how much happier my life has been since I met Lilah and her sisters.

I moved to California on a whim four months ago. To date, it's the single boldest, bravest thing I've ever done. Sometimes I look around and I still can't believe I packed up my beat-up old Honda Civic and drove to California, all alone, with just enough savings to start my business and escape another miserable Minnesota winter.

When I stumbled across the rental listing for the little shop in downtown Sonoma, I just knew it was fate. Even before I left the blustery cold of the Middle River, I could feel the warm California sun on my skin and picture myself driving past miles and miles of picturesque vineyards. I could start fresh and be anyone I wanted to be.

Of course, in my fantasy, I had a convertible, giant sunglasses and endless free time to explore wine country all by myself. The reality of running a business is something else entirely. Long days stuck inside, assembling bookshelves, painting, ordering books, organizing, cleaning, bills, and never-ending paperwork.

3

I'd be miserably lonely if it wasn't for the sisters at the bakery across the road. One week after signing my lease, I put a sign up in my shop window reading:

Coming Soon...
Sorry, I'm Booked!
A Romance Bookstore for Everyone

Within minutes, Olive and Lilah were at my door, ready to break it down if I didn't let them in. That sums up my relationship with the Donovan sisters perfectly. Julia arrived fifteen minutes later, breathless, and declaring that "this better be worth" her break at the hospital. Spoiler alert, she told me later, it was.

I SPEND the next few hours helping customers. Once they clear out, headed home with their newest treasures, I settle down with a happy sigh to eat my salad and finish my book. I spend some time tidying up the shop. I polish the wood counter, sweep the floors, and clean the fingerprints off the glass front door.

Book club starts at seven on the dot. The three Donovan sisters and our friends, Chelsea and Sally, fill the eclectic collection of couches and chairs in the shop's sitting area.

Chelsea and Julia have launched into a heated debate about the motorcycle romance while I top up wine glasses and straighten the cheeseboard Olive brought over.

"It's about vulnerability and overcoming their fear of rejection!" Chelsea all but yells. Judging by the way she's holding her copy of the book, I hope Julia has better catching reflexes than I do.

"I'm just saying, it's not realistic! He's all macho and alpha on his motorcycle, but he's such a pussy about speaking his mind!" Julia argues back.

I decide to keep my feelings to myself, at least for the moment. I love this hero. He's all dirty talk in bed and fiercely possessive of the heroine... but Julia isn't wrong. He is a bit of a pussy when it comes to sharing his emotions. The two of them keep arguing while Olive, Lilah, Sally, and I look on, eyes bouncing between them like it's a tennis match. This happens every month, and I think it boils down to the fact that Julia and Chelsea are just inherent opposites. Chelsea is all sweet innocence. The blushing-bride type living happily ever after with her Prince Charming. Julia is loud, outspoken, spontaneous, and fearlessly living her best life.

God, do I envy her. Moving out here is the only spontaneous thing I've ever done, and it was the best decision of my life. I've got a fresh start. In my new home with my new job, I can be New Parker. Spontaneous Parker. Maybe even Wild Parker... well, probably not. I still have to manage the day-to-day bookstore stuff. It's not like I can go out and party every night. But I can be spontaneous, and I can fight for my own happiness now. That's something Old Parker never had the freedom to do.

The little brass bell over the shop door chimes, pulling me out of my thoughts. Ben, Lilah's fiancé, enters through the narrow, antique door, angling his shoulders to fit properly. He's almost frighteningly large in my opinion, but tiny Lilah adores him. Olive's fiancé, Brooks, follows Ben inside. No shock there. They always pick their women up from book club, but they've abandoned their boys' night earlier than usual and, to my surprise, a third man steps out from behind them.

A tingle of electricity runs through my body, stopping my heart and my breath all in one go. Dark hair falls across part of his face, brushing his cheekbones and obscuring one of his eyes as he purses his lips in an irritated way. He doesn't look at all happy to be here, but that doesn't stop my body from reacting with aching awareness as he leans against the door frame.

Julia is yelling something about someone caving, but she might as well be yelling into a bucket of water for all I'm picking up on. I can't tear my eyes away from him. He's thick and muscular, but not really chiseled. Tattoos cover his arms, disappearing under the sleeves of his tight black t-shirt and trailing all the way down his wrists to the backs of his hands. I can even see some ink peeking out of the collar of his shirt. I wonder what they look like and the thought of him lifting that shirt over his head makes my mouth go dry. There's something sweet

5

about his face and I'm not sure what it is until he meets my eyes and a smirk lifts one corner of his lips. Holy God, his lips are pretty. The pout was nice, but that indolent little smile is staggering.

I'm staring.

I know I am.

But if I thought I couldn't look away before, it's nothing compared to the way I feel when his vibrant green eyes hold mine. Look away? I can't even breathe right. His eyes slowly sweep over my body, shameless, and when his eyebrow lifts appreciatively, I squeak. Like a ridiculous little mouse.

Thankfully, no one hears me because Julia is saying something about drool, scooting her chair back so it screeches on the floor.

"What?" I ask her, ripping my eyes away from the man by the door. My brain clicks back into action, and I realize immediately that he has to be one of the Donovan brothers. The dark hair and bright green eyes are a dead giveaway, and now that my eyes are on Julia and her pouty lips, the family resemblance is unmistakable.

Julia gives me a rueful smile, eyebrow arched, as she says, "Oh, nothing. I'm just going to leave the splash zone before things get icky."

Chelsea spits wine down her front and I must look like a deer in headlights because Julia's face softens a little, as if she regrets teasing me. I feel heat rise in my cheeks as my eyes dart from Julia back to her brother. It must be Lukas with those tattoos. I've heard enough about their brothers to know Asher is too straightedge to have tattoos. Lukas is the troublemaker. That's what Olive says anyway. And he sure as hell looks like a lot of trouble to me.

His little smirk grows into a devastatingly lazy smile. He runs a hand over the shadow covering his jaw and all I can think are dirty thoughts. Best friend's brother or not, I wonder how that scruff would feel scraping my inner thighs. What would it be like to grip his muscular arms as he drove into me?

"Lukas! Out!" Lilah yells as she heads towards him, all but pushing him out the door. He lets her shepherd him outside, but not before giving me a parting wink. Ben follows them, a hand pressed to his mouth and I'm almost positive he's trying to cover a laugh. Looking around the bookshop I realize everyone else is staring at me, eyebrows raised, cocked, scrunched, and lifted.

I feel my cheeks burn as I shrink into myself. I wish they would stop. Why can't they all look at something else? Talk about something, for Christ's sake. I spot Lilah's book on the coffee table, snatch it, and follow her out the door. Anything to escape.

"Lukas, you leave Parker alone." Lilah's voice hits me as I step outside, but Ben's enormous frame is blocking her from my sight.

"Calm your ass, Ladybug," a deep, smokey voice replies. "She's not my type, anyway."

The words hit me like a ton of bricks to the stomach. I feel like a fool. Everyone I know in California just witnessed me have a mental break at the sight of this man. Then they watched him look me up and down and deem me unworthy. That wink was just a parting shot.

I hear him start his motorcycle and drive off. A second later, Lilah turns and sees me, apologizing for her brother.

I do my best to play it off. "It's cool," I say. "For what it's worth, my daddy would hate him."

That's not true, of course. My father, the pastor, doesn't *hate* anyone. He *never* would have let me date a man like that, though. Not that it matters though. A man like Lukas Donovan would never even consider someone like me.

I offer Lilah my most convincing smile, even though I feel cold inside, and hand her the book she forgot. Lilah and Ben leave, walking down the street, his arm wrapped around her protectively. I kind of just want to sit down and cry on the sidewalk but there's a crowd of people right inside my bookshop so I slip on my best *everything-is-perfect* face, take a deep breath and head back inside.

2

LUKAS

"Moping over your missed connection?"

I open one eye and look at my sister, leaning against the doorframe of my office in her blue hospital scrubs. I keep my feet kicked up on my desk, blocking her eyes from my sketchbook, which I slip into my desk drawer before putting my hands behind my head.

"Are you going to use up my entire lunch break to annoy me?" I lean back a little farther, just to emphasize the fact that she's chewing up my free time. Julia sits in the chair opposite mine and there's a thunk as her shoes kick up on the other side of my desk. She gives me a sweetly sarcastic smile, clasping her hands in her lap. Yup. She's definitely here to annoy me. I'm not taking the bait though, so I close my eyes and ignore her. She'll get around to what she wants, eventually.

"So, book club was fun the other night," she says lightly. A muscle twitches in my cheek before I can stop it. Old hawk-eye across the table doesn't miss my tell, and I hear her chuckle.

Fuck.

She snags half of my sandwich off the desk, taking a monstrous bite out of it.

"Do you mind?" I ask my sister, pulling the rest of my food out of her reach. She may be a girl, but I'll still smack her hand if she goes after my peanut butter cup.

"Not at all! This is surprisingly good. I feel like you've upped your sandwich game. Is that chipotle mayo?"

"What do you want, Jules?" I ask, staring up at the ceiling of my office.

"I couldn't help noticing the way you and our sweet little Parker were eyeing each other last night. I'm almost surprised nobody caught a contact pregnancy with the way you were eye-fucking her."

"Jesus, Julia—"

"Oh, don't be a little bitch about it. You were both doing it. I think the sight of you might have made her forget her own name."

"So, you came to warn me off?" I ask, sitting up and scowling at her. "Don't bother. Lilah beat you to it."

My stomach churns as I think about it. Not that she was wrong. I don't have an outstanding track record with her friends. Or women in general. It's not that I'm a bastard about it, I'm just not big on commitment. Why settle for one kind of cake when there are so many to try?

Although I have to admit, Parker looked like really good cake. And I didn't miss the way she looked at me. To be fair, nobody missed it. People three counties over probably felt that intensity. She looked at me like I was the best thing she'd ever seen.

Most people still see me as the fuck-up of the Donovan family. We get a lot of tourists, but this is still a small town. Everyone here knows about the time Joey and I went joyriding in his dad's Tacoma in the ninth grade. They all know I got arrested for drinking in high school.

Granted, the tattoos don't help my public image. But I like tattoos; what's the point of hiding it? Ink or not, I'll always be the trouble-maker, even though it's been more than a decade since I went for a joyride or supposedly broke Sadie Jones' heart. Even a degree in engineering and a thriving business hasn't changed the way people in Sonoma look at me.

Except Parker didn't look at me like that. Her big baby blues burned into me, all heat and admiration. I keep reminding myself that it's only because she hasn't been around long enough to know better. An hour with me would probably be enough to send her cute ass back to Omaha or whatever prairie town she came from.

Julia surprises me by saying, "Oh, I'm not here to warn you off."

"You're not?"

"Hell no! Lilah has a stick up her ass. You'd think Ben would have fixed that by now but—"

"Oh God, please stop." I interrupt her, holding out a hand to stop the Julia train from scarring my brain tissue with mental images I don't need. "I beg you."

Julia rolls her eyes at me but drops her feet to the floor, leaning in conspiratorially.

"Listen, I'm going to tell you something. But if you let Parker know I told you this, I *will* kill you. Got it?" She looks at me, eyebrows raised, waiting.

I give her the Boy Scout salute. "Not a word, I promise," I say sarcastically.

"Parker has a thing for bad boys and motorcycles, and between you and me, I know she's lonely. She's at the bookstore 24/7. She needs some fun."

I blink at her for a moment, sure that I heard her wrong. "I'm sorry," I say finally. "It sounds like you're trying to pimp me out because your friend needs a date."

"Don't be a dick," Julia says, pointing a warning finger at me. "I'm not pimping anyone out. Don't think we missed the way you looked back at her. You can lie to Lilah all you want, but I think Parker is exactly your type. And you're hers. So maybe don't be a pussy about it and go ask her out before someone else gets there first. A curvy little cutie like Parker won't stay on the market long, even if she stays locked in that bookstore forever."

Julia stands to leave but pauses in the doorway, her eyes turned towards the ceiling, false innocence all over her face.

"Lilah has plans with Ben tonight. She said she was leaving the bakery at four… just saying. If you don't want her yelling at you in front of any pretty shopkeepers again, you might want to go downtown later this evening."

"Are you sure that's wise?" I ask her sarcastically. "I mean, what if I break your sweet little friend's heart?"

"*Pfft.* You're a softy and we both know it. I think Parker would be more likely to hurt you than the other way around. She's tougher than she looks..." Julia opens her mouth, tilting her head to the side and squinting one eye, "and sounds."

I mime being stabbed in the heart. "So little faith in me? Not that I'm going over there, but I think I could handle little Parker Thompson."

Julia snorts and turns to leave. She snaps her fingers and turns back around, pointing a finger at me. "Oh! Don't forget Sally's birthday party is Friday night at the bar."

"Like there's any chance you'd let me forget," I sigh.

My baby sister taps her nails on the door frame on her way out. "Love you!" she yells from down the hallway.

"Love you too!" I yell back.

Going back to staring at the ceiling, I mull over what my whirl-wind of a sister said. I don't know if Parker is as tough as Julia thinks. I've heard little bits and pieces about her from my sisters at our family dinners. She's from some podunk town in the Midwest. Her dad was a preacher or something?

I'd be crazy to mess with a girl like that. For one thing, she'd probably try to drag my heathen ass to church. For another, I don't even know how to date a preacher's daughter. I'm not exactly Captain Wholesome. Sure, I'm a good choice for the girls trying to get back at an ex or piss off daddy. I'm a *great* choice if you want someone to make you *scream* "daddy." But I'm not the man you date long term.

Even if Julia is right and Parker has a thing for bad boys, I'd bet my fully restored BMW R75 she's never been with one. She'd probably spend five minutes with me and decide the fantasy was better than the reality.

I'm definitely not going over there. Not tonight. Not ever. It doesn't matter if Parker keeps popping into my thoughts with those curves of hers. It doesn't matter that I want to bury my hands in her strawberry curls and kiss her until she's weak in the knees. It sure as fuck doesn't matter that the idea of someone else laying a finger on her makes me scowl. It's better all around if I keep my distance.

I try to put her out of my head as I settle back into my paperwork. I have to track down a part that is seemingly out of stock everywhere. It takes two hours and unfathomable amounts of swearing, but I finally find it at a little shop down near San Francisco. Checking my watch, I balance the time with the traffic. It's only 2:15 and the drive shouldn't be more than an hour each way. If I leave right now, I can miss the worst of the traffic around the city.

Popping my head into the work bay, I tell Asher what I'm up to.

"Better you than me," he replies with a shrug before rolling back under the SUV he's repairing.

So chatty, that one.

It's too hot for leather but I'm not keen on road rash so I throw my jacket on before fastening my helmet. My bike roars under me as I drive south, the noise and the wind emptying my mind of everything except a certain curvy little redhead. I can't push her out no matter how hard I try. I make it all the way to San Francisco and back, though I'm not sure how since the entire ride flew by in a blur.

I just need to clear my head but as I steer my way toward home, I realize I have to ride past Sorry, I'm Booked to get there. I tell myself I won't even look at it as I go by, but I'm a fucking liar. Beyond the plate glass window, I glimpse Parker behind her counter. She's wearing a dreamy expression, her chin resting on her hand as she stares into space.

Keep driving, I tell myself as I focus back on the quiet street ahead of me.

I make it two whole blocks before I make a sharp turn down an alley and park my bike. I won't go in, I tell myself. I just want to see her. I won't go in.

I backtrack on foot and stand across the street, watching as Parker floats around the shop, dusting and straightening books. She looks… flawless. Coppery curls falling around her shoulders, her eyes are wide and intelligent, and Jesus, those curves. Every step and turn makes her sundress flair around her hips. God himself couldn't have put together a woman more perfectly designed to drive me insane.

Parker frowns to herself as she shelves a stack of books. Her eyebrows are scrunched up, strawberry lips pressed together, not a smile in sight.

I want to see her smile.

3

PARKER

I stare out the window of my shop. The rush is over for the day. The tourists will all be heading out for dinner soon. It was busy for a Wednesday. Actually, it's been busy every day, and the thought makes me smile.

A motorcycle roars by on the road out front and I sit up straight, peering out the plate glass window. The rider, face obscured by a helmet, keeps rolling down the road and I hate that the sound made my heart race. Stupid hormones. I can't believe I just got excited by the thought of seeing Lukas.

Cocky douche.

I mean, I get it. I'm not everyone's cup of tea, but he didn't have to wink at me like he did, adding insult to injury. He made me feel like a joke, and there's not much in the world that makes me feel worse. My cheeks burn just thinking about it.

Standing up and stepping out from behind the counter, I shake it off. I did nothing wrong. It's not my fault he was rude. Eyeing myself in the mirror, I fix my hair and straighten my shoulders. I won't let him get to me. And I won't get excited every time I hear a motorcycle outside.

Maybe.

I work my way around the shop, dusting the shelves and straightening books. I'm in the back of the shop when I hear the bell twinkle over the front door.

"Be right with you!" I call out as I shelve a rogue book.

"No rush," comes a deep, teasing voice from the front. Not the kind of voice I'm used to in here. My clientele is almost all women with the occasional husband dragged along to sulk quietly in the corner.

Peeking out around the edge of the shelf, my eyes go wide. The man has his back to me, jeans and a tight black t-shirt showcasing broad shoulders and a really great butt. It's official. My love of romance books has turned me into a total pervert. *Peeping on customers from behind shelves*, I think, shaking my head at myself. Cute rear end or no, that's just wrong. I'm probably creeping on somebody's husband.

Still scolding myself, I step out to help him but then he turns, looking around the shop idly and there's no mistaking that face, even in profile. Ducking back behind the shelf, I clutch the book in my hands to my chest like it could shield me from the sexiest, most infuriating man on the planet.

What in the sweet hell is Lukas Donovan doing here? Surely, he's lost... right?

Jesus. Just because I like looking at him doesn't mean I want to *see* him, especially after the humiliation of last weekend. I wonder how long I can hide back here before he either leaves or comes looking for me. I can't make it to the backroom without him seeing me.

He places his hands on my counter, leaning forward and making the muscles in his forearms flex. I have to swallow the whimper I feel in my throat. It appears he's going to make himself right at home and do his absolute best to make me melt in the process. I don't see any way out of this... I'm going to have to interact with him.

I steel myself. I will *not* give him the satisfaction of knowing how my heart races at the sight of him. Do I yearn to lean into that broad chest and see if he smells as good as he looks? Hell yes.

But I am a professional, dammit.

I wince as I step out from behind the shelf. I'm not great with men in general and I have a sneaking suspicion that this could go very badly.

Lukas glances over and grins at me as I get closer. I veer to the side, heading behind the counter, and putting as much space between us as I can. All while doing my very best to ignore the way his devilish smile makes my panties damp.

I stare at him for a second, trying to make my mouth work right.

"Wh-What can I help you with, Mr. Donovan?" I ask, pleased that by the end of the sentence I hardly sound breathy at all.

Lukas laughs softly. "You can call me Lukas, you know. Do you call my sisters Ms. Donovan?"

"No. But they're my friends. I don't really know you, do I?" I reply.

"We could be friends," he says casually. His eyes flick down over my body, and I get lost in him for one pulse-thumping second as heat flares through my body, equal parts desire, and anger. Friends? Really? He has some nerve! I mean yeah, he's pretty and I enjoy looking at him... maybe even fantasize about the way his lips would feel trailing down my neck... but I'm not exactly dying to be friends with the kind of douche canoe who embarrasses women for fun.

He taps his fingertips on the worn book on the counter, eyeing the glossy cover and the tattooed, shirtless man on a motorcycle. I snatch it up and tuck it under the counter.

"That's not for sale," I tell him quickly.

"You like guys on bikes?" he asks, lips quirked. His green eyes are practically dancing with mischief.

Unbelievable! Did he come to my shop just to make fun of me? I press my lips together so I don't say something rude. Anger spreads through me and I take several breaths through my nose, trying to calm myself. It doesn't work well, but I have a modicum of control when I answer.

"Not even a little. That was just for book club," I say, jutting out my chin.

He grins and squints one eye at me like he doesn't believe a word I'm saying. "But I thought you picked the books. That's what my sister said."

Lukas plunks a key on my defunct typewriter. It makes a clunk before the arm sticks. Out of instinct, I reach out and carefully lower it before pushing his hand away. The pads of my fingers tingle where they touched his and I yank it back, making a fist at my side. Definitely no touching. Not if I want to keep my dignity intact.

"That's broken," I say unnecessarily.

"I see that," Lukas says, his smile pulling up on one side, smirking at me. His green eyes sweep over my face as he leans closer. "You have freckles."

I freeze, staring at him and blinking. "Yes… Can I help you with something?" I ask, truly confused. Did he really come here just to rub in how much I'm not his type? That seems unnecessarily cruel.

He runs a hand over his jaw, the bristles of his short beard rasping quietly as he watches my face, still smiling at me.

"Yeah, I think you can, Parker. I want a book."

"Ooookay…" I answer slowly. "For whom?"

"For me."

There is a lot of blinking going on right now. How much do I normally blink? Because this seems excessive. I tap my fingers against my leg and get a hold of myself.

"This is a *romance* bookstore. Are you a big fan of romance novels, Mr. Donovan?"

"I told you to call me Lukas. And I've never read one, so you get to pop my cherry." He grins at me, cocky as all hell and I *hate* that it looks so good on him.

I'm sure my eyes bug out of my head, despite my best efforts not to react. Because that's what he wants, right? To get a rise out of me? To shock the sweet little midwestern girl with his dirty mouth? Oh God that mouth… I read dirty romances all day long but when the living, breathing embodiment of my fantasies says something like that, it's hard to keep a poker face.

"Great," I squeak. "How about science fiction?"

He chuckles, rubbing his hand through his beard again, distracting me. "Sure. Pick something for me."

17

4

LUKAS

I almost feel guilty for making Parker so flustered. I mean, the cherry popping thing was low-hanging fruit, but even though I know it wasn't fair, I can't find it in me to feel bad about it. Maybe that makes me a bastard. A decent guy wouldn't have said it, but the pink rising behind her freckles is one of the sexiest things I've ever seen, and blushing is one step up from the wary look she's been giving me since I walked in here.

She can try to frown all she wants, but I didn't miss the heat that flared in her eyes before her cheeks went up in blazes. Hell, the blush spread all the way down her collarbone and under the neckline of her dress. I bet she blushes in bed too. Her skin would probably go all flushed and pink as she comes…

Parker hurries around the counter, giving me a wide berth as she heads to a shelf near the front of the store. She watches me out of the corner of her eye, tracking me like she's worried about letting me out of her sight. I follow her, enjoying the way her hips sway in that little sundress. The little cherry print looks almost as juicy as she does.

She reaches up to grab a book off the bookshelf and holds it close to her chest.

"You seriously want to read a romance book?" she asks me.

I step closer, not enough to be threatening but enough that she has to tip her head back to look up at me. Close enough to smell the clean scent of her laundry and a hint of peaches. I lean forward another inch, breathing her in.

I couldn't care less which book she gives me at this point.

"Yep... why else would I be here, Freckles?" I grin at her, watching her pupils dilate and contract in her ocean blue eyes. She holds her breath before huffing at me, her pretty eyebrows scrunching up again.

"It's on the house." The words rush out of her as she shoves the book into my chest and, breasts heaving, pushes me towards the door. My fingers tangle with hers as I hold both the book and her hands against my chest. I let her move me, mostly because the little scowl she is wearing is adorable.

"You have to let me pay for it," I protest. My back hits the door with a thump and she reaches around me, momentarily pressing her front against mine, her soft curves molded to my torso as she turns the door handle.

"Sorry, we're closed!" she says as my feet hit the pavement. Her hands extricate themselves from mine and she leaves me outside in the evening sun, holding the book.

"Is this because I called you Freckles?" I ask with a laugh.

"No, this is because I don't like you," Parker says as she shuts the door in my face.

"Liar," I call out as she locks the door and disappears into the back of the shop.

An older couple passes by, throwing me some serious side-eye. I'm sure we just made quite the scene. Curvy little Parker shoving a big, tattooed man out the door of a romance bookshop would probably be enough, but I realize that I'm clutching a book with a mostly naked green bodybuilder on the cover.

I offer the couple a brief salute and head back down the street toward my bike. I've got some reading to do.

5

PARKER

Friday night rolls around with as much speed as a sloth on Ambien. I watch the clock all day, anxious to close up and get to Sally's birthday celebration. Her carefully chosen present is already wrapped up and waiting in the back of my car.

I haven't seen hide nor hair of Lukas Donovan since he blindsided me the other day. Which is a good thing, since the more I think about the way he made fun of me and teased me about my freckles, the angrier I get. If he turns back up in my store, I'll probably flip out on him, and nobody wants to see that.

I've gotten myself worked up with comebacks I wish I'd thought of before. Now I'm itching for Lukas to show up, just so I can tell him off. I get a little thrill of anticipation anytime an engine roars by outside on Main Street, but it's never him. So, I just save up all the sassy retorts in a mental catalog labeled: "Use to Eviscerate Lukas Donovan."

The list is getting so long I'd probably need at least three sightings to use them all. Some of them are rather specific, but there's no way I'm going to let him catch me off guard again. The armor is in place, metaphorically.

I lock up right at closing time, double checking the locks before walking to the municipal lot where I park my Civic. It starts right up, with only a minor rattle and a little thunk, and I pat the dashboard affectionately. This baby has seen better days. It was a beater when I bought it in high school, and at this point, it's mostly held together by the faded paint job. But she keeps holding on, year after year; as long as I top up the oil every other week. And I really can't complain because I couldn't afford to replace it and still make rent.

Driving home with the windows down makes everything else go away. I swear, I'll never tire of the wineries and golden sunshine. I park on the street and walk around the side of my landlord's house to the back gate. The chain-link fence rattles as I fight with the latch. It's bent just enough to make it impossible to open with one hand. I get it open and slam it closed again once I'm in the backyard.

A black mass slams into the fence from the neighbor's side. A hundred and fifty pounds of terrifying muscle barks at me, scaring the ever-loving shit out of me and sending my heart slamming around in my chest.

"Down, Cujo!" I gasp. You'd think I'd be used to the darn Rottweiler by now, but he's stealthy! He sneaks up on me on purpose, I know it. I dig in my purse, pulling out the crust of bread I saved from my lunch, and toss it over the fence. He chases after it, his short little tail wiggling in excitement. I watch him wolf it down and trot back to the fence. This time he gives a little hop and lands his front paws up on the top bar of the fence, a puppy smile on his big drooling face. He's wiggling so hard it makes his paws dance around.

I rub his ears and scratch around his collar while he makes chuffing noises at me and licks my face. "Who's a good boy?" I baby talk. He's a big softy, even if he likes to scare the pants off of me. Cujo dances harder and snuffles in my ear when I hug his colossal head. I've always wanted a dog but having him next door is as close as I can get right now.

"Go play," I say, shooing him off the fence before heading inside.

My place is a one room backyard... bungalow? Bungalow sounds cuter than shed, but it sort of implies more space. I guess it's like an old-school version of a tiny home. Let's go with that. Anyway, my tiny home has a mini kitchenette, a little closet of a bathroom with the world's dinkiest shower, and a loft bed. The elderly couple who own it tried to use it as an Airbnb, but the neighborhood sucks and it's too far from downtown to be ideal for tourists. It's fine for me, though. I don't mind a bit of a drive and I literally couldn't find anything cheaper.

Inside, I hang my purse on the hook and start a pot of coffee. When it comes to partying, I can't keep up with Sally and Julia without caffeine, it's just a fact of life. I spread peanut butter on a piece of bread, fold it in half and take a big bite while I watch the coffee drip into the pot. It's a sad little dinner, but it's what I've got for now. I *really* need to go grocery shopping, but I'm tight on money until next week. At least I have half and half for the coffee.

I flick through my pitiful clothes rack, trying to decide what to wear. My options are… limited. I left most of my old clothes behind when I bolted. As far as I'm concerned, Puritanical floor-length skirts and turtlenecks have no place in California, but the bookstore has chewed up almost every cent I have. It's a necessary sacrifice, and I'll subsist on my meager collection of Walmart clearance rack finds for as long as it takes.

I land on a fluttery pink tank top and a pair of white denim shorts that I haven't been brave enough to wear yet. I usually wear jeans but it's so flipping hot out; I think I might melt in that much denim. Slipping my feet into my (only) pair of cute sandals, I throw back the last sip of coffee before washing my mug and straightening up the kitchenette.

I pull my hair up in a messy bun and check it in the mirror by the door. It's way too hot to wear it down tonight. I don't care if the bar is air conditioned or not; if we spend more than five minutes outside, I'll be a sweaty mess.

For all the minor annoyances of my shed—I mean tiny home— one of the big benefits is that a single baby air conditioner does a great job at keeping it a comfortable temperature. The sun is setting as I leave, but I'm hit hard by a wave of heat the second I open the door.

I'm definitely not a summer girl, but a hot day in California still beats the hell out of any day back in Middle River. I might live in a closet and sweat constantly, but it's all worth it to have the freedom to come and go as I please. To read anything I want without hiding my books under the floorboards. Plus, you can't argue with the views out here.

The drive back to Main Street is quick. I find a parking spot two blocks from the bar where I'm supposed to meet the Donovan sisters and Sally. I'm out of my car and halfway down the street before I remember Sally's gift and have to run back. I special ordered the box set just for her and can't wait to see her face when she sees it.

The light in the bar is dim, even compared to the twilight outside, but once my eyes adjust, it's impossible to miss Sally. She's wearing a tight black dress and her hair is a shocking shade of pink this week. She wouldn't tell me how old she was the last time I asked. She just said "twenty-nine" and winked at me. I'm guessing she's been twenty-nine for the last thirty years, but age is more about how you feel, right?

"Parker!" Sally yells from her spot on the dance floor. She waves wildly for me to join her. Lilah and Ben are dancing nearby while Olive and Brooks are at the bar. They all cheer my name in chorus and it makes me blush. I'm not used to getting this much attention, but it's sweet and I'm learning to love it.

When I don't join Sally on the dance floor, she barrels over to me.

"Get your cute butt out here!" Her voice is muffled by the music and the clink of glasses behind the bar. I shake my head because I really need some liquid courage before I brave dancing in public. She wraps me in a mama-bear hug and it feels so good. I didn't exactly get a lot of hugs from my parents growing up and I have to admit, I want to bask in Sally's affection like a turtle in the sunshine.

She releases me and looks me up and down, holding me at arm's length, her eyebrows raised. "What are you wearing?"

"You don't like it?" I know my clothes are cheap, but I thought I looked cute.

"Oh, I like it, but you look like a juicy little chicken that just wandered into a wolf den."

"I brought you a present!" I tell her, desperately trying to change the subject.

"You didn't need to do that!" she says before holding out her hand. "But gimme!"

I laugh and give her the bag, watching with glee as she rips into

23

the tissue paper and pulls out a filthy series of books featuring a group of cougars finding their happily ever afters with hunky billionaires. Sally cackles and hugs the box set to her chest.

"I love you, baby girl!" she shouts over the music before kissing me on the cheek. "Come on, I'm buying you a drink."

"But it's your birthday," I argue. "I should buy you one, not the other way around."

Sally gives me a stern look. "Listen here, girlie. I opened my own business too. I remember what it was like in the early days. You can buy me a drink next year when your bookshop is making more money than you can handle. For now, you let your friends help you when they want to. Got it?"

"Yes, ma'am," I say with a quivery lip. I forget sometimes that Sally struck out on her own too. She orders each of us a shot of tequila and a margarita. She licks salt off her hand, tosses her shot back, slamming her glass down on the bar before sucking on a lime wedge.

I've never done a shot of tequila before, but I've seen it done and Sally makes it look like it's no big deal. I can do this, right? Totally. *How bad could it be?* I think as I flinch and throw the shot back. *Really flipping bad!* It burns like acid death in my throat, making me choke and gasp for breath.

"Oh, gosh damn!" I sputter. "That is *horrible!*" I say, trying not to gag.

"Oh, pumpkin! Haven't you had tequila before?" Sally asks, rubbing my back.

"In margaritas," I wheeze. "It's not very good straight, though."

Sally chuckles. "Oh, I don't know. I feel pretty good!"

"That's because you're immune," Lilah says from behind Sally, making her laugh.

"I'm dancing!" Sally yells, pulling on my hand.

"I'll be right there," I tell her. *Once I get the battery acid out of my mouth*, I add silently.

Lilah eyes my margarita as she sips a seltzer. "You can have it," I tell her slyly.

"No," she sighs. "I really can't. But thank you!"

Oh, yeah. She's definitely preggers. I wonder how long she's going

24

to keep it a secret. With her sisters and Gran around, I doubt it will last long.

Lilah slides the margarita closer to me. "Enjoy it! Just don't try to go drink-for-drink with Sally. She'll wreck you. Ask me how I know."

Ben steps up behind her and I pretend I don't see the huge hand he slides over her stomach or the way she blushes when he whispers in her ear. I've heard enough stories to know they are absolutely filthy together. #Relationshipgoals, right?

I let Lilah convince me to join her and Sally on the dance floor. For better or worse, the tequila did its job.

6

LUKAS

I'm late. But I'm always late, so I doubt anyone will care that I'm rolling up to the bar an hour after the party started. My sister Julia is out front having a heated conversation on her cell phone. Her voice filters through the street noise as I cut the engine and take my helmet off.

"… and I told you, I'm not covering for an incompetent doctor. He needs to get his head out of his ass or I'll go to the administration. I know he thinks his shit doesn't stink but I-hello?" She looks at her phone, rage clouding her face. "Asshole," she mutters at the dark phone as I approach.

"Hospital?" I ask.

She nods. "I hate incompetence."

I toss my arm around her shoulder and steer her inside. "I know. Come on, I'll buy you a beer."

"Two," Julia haggles as we step inside.

"You drive a hard bargain, but I accept your terms," I say. The bartender eyes my sister until he realizes I'm giving him a murderous glare. He brings our beers back, eyes averted. I take mine and turn on my barstool to eye the party. Gran is shaking it next to Sally and laughing as the birthday girl blows a kiss at a group of the guys.

26

And there, dancing between Olive and Lilah is Parker. She's swinging her hips and laughing while balancing half a margarita in one hand. She has her hair piled up on top of her head and little strands have escaped, curling against her sweat-dampened neck. Her pink tank top makes her look like a flower. Even from here, I can see the freckles that kiss her cheeks and speckle her shoulders and chest.

And sweet fucking Jesus. She's wearing little white shorts, exposing so much leg that it's driving me nuts. Those shorts are damn near indecent and all I can imagine is pulling her over here to straddle my lap. I want to kiss her senseless with those legs wrapped around me, grinding against my aching cock.

Everywhere I look, men are watching her dance. Watching the way her ass shakes in those damn shorts and probably thinking even worse than me. Her movements make her tank top swing and shift, teasing views of cleavage that I can barely rip my eyes away from. I'm torn between never wanting her to stop and needing to level anyone who dares to look at her.

Julia chuckles quietly, and I glance up to find her watching me.

"Yeah, totally not your type. You're a terrible fucking liar, Lukas."

"Shut up," I say, then grudgingly admit, "I know." I'm all for modern women, but it bothers me she's out here all alone. Is anyone watching out for her at all? The frustration simmers in my blood as I glare at a middle-aged guy down the bar with a biker jacket and grizzled beard. He's watching Parker like she's a tasty snack. She seems unaware of him until she looks up and the disgusting bastard licks his lips and winks at her.

She visibly shrinks, cringing back behind my sisters and Sally. The simmering annoyance erupts into a boil. Nobody is going to make her feel unsafe. Nobody.

Kicking my bar stool backwards with a screech, I stand and step in front of El Douche, blocking his view of Parker and my sisters. I don't yell. Yelling does nothing, in my experience. Instead, I draw myself up to my full height and lean over him, slapping a $20 bill on the bar. In my most menacing voice, I say, "Looks like you're all paid up. Get the fuck out."

El Douche might have been disgustingly brave with Parker, but apparently, he's not in the mood to tangle with me. I have several inches and plenty of muscle on him and based on the throat clearing behind me, I've got back up from my future brothers-in-law. El Douche stands, puffing up his chest.

"No harm in lookin'," he grumps.

Rage floods my bloodstream, my heart trying to punch its way out of my rib cage. I lunge at him and grab him by the collar of his smelly jacket and shake him as I whisper through my teeth, "You're gonna feel plenty of harm unless you keep your eyes to your fucking self from now on."

A soft hand on my arm pulls me back half an inch, and I let El Douche go with a little shove. He backs up to the door, raising his eyebrows at me once before leaving.

I watch to make sure he's really gone, stretching my neck and rolling my shoulders to relieve some of the tension that's cinching up my muscles. When I turn, I expect to see one of my sisters or maybe Sally, but the hand on my bicep is creamy and smooth with little tan freckles. I look up and Parker's bright blue eyes are wide in her face, alarm etched in every curve. Great. I fucking scared her.

"It's not worth hitting him over," she says quietly. Not worth it? Is she fucking serious?

"What are you talking about, Parker? He had it coming. It'll be a snowy day in hell when I let a piece of shit get away with eye-fucking you like that."

My voice comes out harsher than I meant it to, and Parker pulls her hand away so fast you'd think I burned her.

"Go dance," I tell her gruffly.

Her eyes drop to the floor, and my stomach goes with them. She's so fucking sweet and I'm an asshole. The last thing I need is to get arrested for assault, but I couldn't stand his eyes on her and I sure as hell won't stand by while anyone makes a woman feel less than safe. I try to find it in me to feel sorry for causing a scene, but I can't.

"Yeah... thanks for standing up for me," she mumbles before turning and heading back to my sisters.

The party picks back up, but there's a shift in the air. I've made everyone wary, and Parker's eyes keep darting in my direction before sliding away just as quickly. She's probably just waiting for me to explode again. I feel like a dick, but I can't say I wouldn't do it again.

7

PARKER

I rejoin my friends on the dance floor, but my heart isn't in it anymore. I keep replaying the way Lukas grabbed that guy and shook him. All because the guy winked at me and licked his lips. I mean, the guy was revolting, sure, but I'm still shocked that Lukas stood up for me. I can't remember anyone standing up for me... well, ever. I'm sure he only did it because I'm here with his sisters. I know he watches out for them too.

But even more surprising than witnessing him lunge at that guy was the way my body reacted. I grabbed him so he wouldn't hit the guy and get in trouble, but part of me *loved* seeing him get aggressive like that. The downstairs parts of me particularly loved it and I know I'm going to be replaying that all night even if it sends me straight to hell. He is insanely good at fulfilling my motorcycle bad boy fantasy. And even though I know that blow up wasn't really about *me*, I can pretend it was. Possessive Lukas is better vibrator fodder than any romance novel. I shiver just remembering the way his arm muscles flexed as he grabbed that guy's jacket.

Wow. There is something *seriously* wrong with me.

Lukas is still at the bar an hour later. He's sitting sideways, nursing a beer, and it looks like he's beating himself up. When he drops his chin like that, his hair falls in his eyes and I want to brush it back. Never mind the fact that I'm not his type, he doesn't like my freckles, and I'm probably too curvy for his taste. It's a cruel twist of fate that I'm so drawn to him. What is it? Pheromones? Daddy issues? Long-neglected lady bits? Whatever it is, it's a total dick, has terrible taste, and doesn't care about my fragile ego at all.

But he looks so down on himself… Ugh. Fine.

I cross to the bar and sit next to him. The bartender practically trips in his hurry to take my drink order. *See?* I think to myself. At least some guys find me attractive. I've already had plenty to drink, so I order water and return the bartender's smile half-heartedly.

"This is a bar, you know," Lukas says, staring down at the beer in his hand. He holds it precariously between a couple of fingers, fidgeting with the label as the bartender drops my water off.

"Yes, I know. But look! They serve water too! Amazing," I say sarcastically. I sip the water through a metal straw and close my eyes as the pleasure of the icy coolness slides down my parched throat.

Lukas eyes my mouth for a second before looking back at his beer.

"You're kind of mouthy for such a sweet girl."

I narrow my eyes at him. "You don't know anything about me."

He laughs mirthlessly. "Oh, I bet I know more than you think." He stares straight ahead, a small smile tugging up the corner of his lips. It's all I can manage not to stare at them. I'm finding his attitude incredibly annoying… even if I grudgingly admit that I enjoy sitting next to him. Even so, he's spent all of ten minutes in my shop and he thinks he knows me? Bull crap. He knows nothing.

"Try me," I challenge him, the tequila making me braver than usual. This is all part of New Spontaneous Parker.

Lukas sets his beer down on the bar, turning his body towards me and straightening on his stool. His fingers trace the curve of the beer bottle as he looks me up and down, assessing me and I'm forcibly reminded of the first night we met; his eyes hot as he took in every inch of me and then declared me "not his type."

"Let's see. You're out on your own for the first time. Just got out from under Mommy and Daddy's thumb and you're riding that wave of newfound freedom. How am I doing so far?" he asks with a smirk.

31

My mouth hangs open because, while he's not wrong, his tone of voice is so condescending. He makes me sound like some pathetic backwoods girl, too naïve to take care of herself. I open my mouth to tell him he's way off, but he interrupts me.

"You know what I think, Parker? I think the preacher's daughter wants to break bad and slum it with a biker. I think you've heard just enough to know I've got a bad reputation. Or, rather, an excellent reputation from where you're sitting because I think you want to see what it's like to get fucked before you inevitably settle down with a Ken Doll. How am I doing here?"

Heat races over my face and down my chest, the blush spreading over my entire body. The sheer nerve of talking to me like that! I sputter, too angry to make coherent sentences, but I hold his eyes, refusing to look away. That's what he wants, right? To make me feel like less?

"How dare you," I reply with quiet anger. My breath heaves as I grip the water glass so hard my fingers hurt. "You don't know a flipping thing about me. I just came to sit next to you because you looked unhappy and I thought you'd like the company. That's what I get for being nice to you, huh? Insulted? Made fun of? You just proved how little you know about me."

I lean closer, anger and tequila making me extra 'mouthy,' as he puts it. "And for your information, I've *been* fucked, not that it's really any of your business."

He doesn't quell when I whisper-yell in his face. He stands and leans over me, one forearm propped on the bar, casual as can be. I'm so... *aware* of Lukas. I hate this physical pull I feel towards him. He's big and thick, and I bet he'd be amazing if he wasn't such a raging asshole.

He puts his face right down next to mine, his green eyes piercing me, as he says, "Nah, baby girl. I bet men make love to you. Slowly, sweetly, in missionary position, with the lights off."

Furious, I turn on my stool and hop off. "I guess that's what you'd expect. I mean, *you* might need the lights off just to get it up since I'm so not your type."

I try not to take extra joy in the shocked expression on his face when I walk away. Let him choke on that. New Parker kicks ass.

32

WORK DRAGS by the next day. The only bright spot is the group of Canadian grandmas who clean out my historical section. I have way too much time to replay my conversation with Lukas. I guess it was more of a fight. Whatever you call it, he struck a nerve in a big way.

Despite his obnoxious attitude and tone of voice, he wasn't completely wrong about me, which is probably the thing I hate most. I am definitely enjoying my newfound freedom, but what's so bad about that? He didn't grow up in a cold, ultra-religious house with parents that didn't love each other or their kid. He didn't live in a pressure cooker, shut off from his peers. If he'd had a life like mine, he'd embrace the freedom too.

And the sex thing. He didn't have to be such a bastard about it, did he? Maybe I don't have a ton of experience, but honestly, sex is over-rated. I'd rather read a book and take care of myself, anyway.

And what's wrong with having the lights off? That's normal, isn't it? I don't know. I mean, I've read plenty, but that's not the same as genuine experience, is it? I've had sex exactly once, and it was so awful, so disappointing, that I never wanted a repeat.

Angry, I set my teacup down a little too hard. The ancient porcelain cracks and the last of my cold Earl Grey spills across the counter.

"Shit," I yelp, scrambling to save my book from the spreading tea before grabbing a handful of tissues. I sweep the mess into the trash, soggy tissues, broken cup and all. I growl in the back of my throat. That was my only teacup. I have one mug back at home, but I need that for coffee. Now I have to go out and buy a stupid cup and it won't be as cute as my vintage one. Maybe I'll get lucky at the thrift store.

Today sucks. I close up right at 5 pm. Sometimes I hang out a little longer because tourists will wander in after dinner if I'm still open, but tonight I just want to go home. I'm going to get in my pajamas, make some ramen for dinner, watch a movie on my phone, and fall asleep before the sun even sets. No shame, that sounds awesome right now.

I'm only five minutes from downtown when my car makes a clunk. Not a little "you-hit-a-pothole-too-hard" clunk. This is a *CLUNK.*

33

And then there's a horrifying grinding sound accompanied by billowing smoke from under the hood of the Civic.

I manage to pull the car off the road before it stops, but it's a near miracle. I'm shaking with adrenaline as I grab my purse and jump out of the car, probably setting a new land speed record. I don't know much about cars, but smoke is never a good sign, right?

Once I'm at a safe distance, at least I hope it's a safe distance, I try to filter through my options. I'm broke. Towing is going to cost an arm and a leg and repairs will take the other half of me. I am so completely, royally screwed.

Screaming out at the picturesque vineyard behind the car, I give in to the urge to throw a temper tantrum. I kick the gravel that covers the shoulder of the road and heave an angry breath before getting myself under control.

My options are few and not very palatable. Sighing, I call Lilah. I run my hands through my hair as the phone rings. She finally answers and her voice is breathless as she says, "Hey Parker!"

Oh god, I hope I didn't interrupt something. Yikes.

"Hey, I'm so sorry to bug you. I-I'm stranded."

"Oh my God, where? What happened?" she asks. I can hear Ben in the background asking her what's wrong.

"Um… I'm like five minutes outside of town. My car broke down. It's bad. There was grinding and clunking and now it's smoking."

"Wait, is it smoke or steam?"

I peer at the car without getting closer. "I have no clue… maybe steam?"

Lilah groans. "What do I know? I don't even know why I'm asking. I'll send Asher to help, ok? He's closest and he can tow your car back to the shop."

"Wait—" my voice cracks. "Do you think he'll let me work out a payment plan or something? I don't think I can pay him today." I actually *know* that I can't pay him right now, but my pride is damaged enough standing here on the side of the road with my car billowing smoke as cars creep by, curious faces pressed to the windows. Smoke or steam. Either way, it's a death sentence for the car. There's no way it's worth repairing.

"Oh my God, he'll do it for free. There's no way I'd let him charge you! Don't worry about a thing, Parker. We've got you."

Tears well up in my eyes as I thank her. "I'll pay him back," I promise. I'm not a charity case, but I'm also not stupid enough to look the gift horse in the mouth when I'm being offered a reprieve.

"*Pfft*, stop. Don't worry about it! Just hang on. I'll go call Asher right now. Give me your location and he'll be there in a couple minutes."

8

LUKAS

Why did I have to push her away like that? Jesus. The look on Parker's face last night was pure fire and I have to admit, it was as sexy as it was shocking. She's usually all blushes and deer-in-the-headlights eyes, but the way she threw her shoulders back and told me off… fuck.

I get an uncomfortable twist in my stomach when I think about that last comment: "Since I'm so not your type."

Hearing her say that out loud was like a dagger shoved between my ribs. I doubt it's a coincidence that those are the words she used. The universe isn't that kind. I don't know where she heard it, but I'm fucking kicking myself. I just wanted Lilah off my ass, and now that's what Parker thinks of me. I drag a hand through my hair. Typical. Speak without thinking, act without planning. That's just me to a T, isn't it?

Asher's phone rings on the other side of the bay but he's with a customer so I ignore it. Until it starts back up with his annoying ass ringtone. Sighing and muttering curses under my breath, I slide out from under the car I'm working on, but Asher runs across the garage to answer it.

"You could put that shit on vibrate, you know!" I call out as he answers it, silently flipping me the bird. I sit up and grin at my grumpy older brother.

"Hey, Ladybug. What's up? ... Ah, fuck. Where is she? ... Wait, is it smoke or steam? ... Well, is it on fire? ... Yes, it matters very much... Because I can deal with one and the other requires the fire department... No, I'm not being sarcastic... Okay, just text me her number and location. I'll leave now."

"Who's stranded?" I ask Asher. A little tingle of worry crawls up my spine, because I've seen (and heard) that piece of shit Parker drives around. I don't know how it's still running at this point. I can tell you just by listening to it that it needs new belts, an overhaul on the suspension, an alignment, the transmission is failing, and the wheel bearings are shot. I can't even imagine how bad it is under the hood.

"Parker. Her car broke down on the side of Petaluma heading out of town."

"Shit, radiator?"

"Sounds like it. Lilah said she's covering repairs."

"Repairs?" I laugh. "She needs a new fucking car."

Asher shrugs, apathetic, or maybe just not in the mood to fight about it right now. "Either way, I'm going to take the tow truck and pick her up."

I jump up, the creeper seat flying out from under me and lodging under another car. "I've got it," I tell him, heading for the keys, but he steps in front of me.

"Hold up," he says. "Lilah asked me to go. In fact, she specifically told me not to let you pick up Parker. I don't get involved in shit the way the girls do, but I heard you were a Grade A dick last night."

"Don't worry," I assure. "I've got this. Text me the info." I snag the tow truck keys off the hook and jog to the wrecker.

"You better not tell Lilah!" he yells after me.

The sick feeling in my stomach eases up for the first time today and the closer I get to Petaluma the better I feel. I'm practically bouncing in my seat by the time I see her car pulled over onto the shoulder. The good feeling evaporates when I spot Parker sitting a good distance from the car on the gravel shoulder. She has her knees tucked up, hugging them, her head resting on her forearms. She looks so small and sad. And even from a distance, I can see the tear tracks on her cheeks.

She perks up when I pull in in front of the Honda, squinting at the sunlight reflecting off my windshield, relief smoothing the lines on her face. That is until I open the door and step out of the cab.

"You have got to be flipping kidding me! Why are you here? Lilah said Asher was coming!" she yells, wiping the tears from her face furiously.

"Well, you got me," I reply as I circle the Honda, looking at her out of the corner of my eye. The soft white tank top hugs her curves, her breasts peeking out the top. I have to bite my lip to drag my eyes (and indecent thoughts) away from her and focus on the car. Steam is still coming from under the hood. It's definitely not smoke and the damn thing isn't on fire, so that's good.

"What happened?" I ask as I approach her and hold out a hand to help her up. It's only now that I'm realizing how dirty I am. My hands are coated in grease and I ran out of the shop in my work coveralls. I'm sure I look every inch the grease monkey.

Parker glares at my hand and then up at me, before standing on her own, eyebrows scrunched in a stubborn expression. I get the impression that's just her personal aversion to me and less about the state of my hands. Her baby blues hold mine for a beat and I get a hint of that juicy peach smell that seems to float around her. Whether it's the way she smells like heaven, even on the side of a dusty road, or the defiant look in her eyes, I don't know, but my dick stirs in my jeans. Real bad timing, bud.

Parker breaks the eye contact first, turning her scowl toward the car. "I don't know. There was a big clunk, and then a 'gkgkgkgk,' something screeched, and then the smoke." She talks with her hands, miming an explosion before letting her hands fall to her hips. I fight the urge to smile at her description of the sounds, but it's hard. She's cute as hell.

"I barely pulled it off the road before it gave out. I called Lilah, who told me she would send Asher. Then, much to my dismay, you turned up instead."

There we go. That comment took care of any temptation I had to

38

smile. Interestingly, it does nothing to abate the half-chub I'm concealing. Fuck. This is going so much worse than I had expected. I mean, I
guess I didn't expect her to be thrilled to see me; I'm not exactly her
favorite person right now. But I came to rescue her. That counts for
something, right?

"Parker, I'm sorry about the way I talked to you last night. I was
out of line."

She pauses, taken aback, opening and closing her mouth like she
wants to say something but isn't sure what.

"The A/C is on in the cab," I tell her. "Why don't you wait in there
while I get your car set up."

Parker eyes me suspiciously, sweeping her long hair off of her neck.
I follow the movement and watch as a little bead of sweat trails down
her neck, along the swell of her breast, and down the front of her shirt.
It takes everything in me not to haul her against me and trace its path
with my tongue. I swallow and blink, shoving the impulse as far down
as I can, but when I meet her eyes, the suspicion is gone, replaced with
that wide-eyed innocent look I like so much.

"Right," she says. "Truck."

I clear my throat and nod. She drops her eyes and heads for the
passenger seat as I move to the back of the truck. I watch her walk over
to the truck and climb up, her jeans showing off every glorious curve
as she moves.

Averting my eyes from that glorious ass, I try to get my head back
on the job. It's not like it's hard to tow a car, but I don't want to make
a stupid mistake because I'm fixated on the little redhead in my truck.

I lower the bed and tilt it down, hooking the chains to the frame
before tightening them up, all the while being careful not to burn
myself on the hot metal or let the condensation drip on me. Her radiator is completely shot, there's a burning rubber smell that I suspect is
coming from the engine belt, and I'm willing to bet the engine over-
heated. Lilah might have offered to pay for repairs, but I suspect a
whole new car would cost less.

I get the little Honda winched up onto the bed and strapped
down, double-checking the safety points before climbing back up in
the cab with Parker. The cool air feels amazing, but even better is the

sight of her strawberry hair ruffling in the breeze from the vent. She eyes me warily, and I do my best not to stare at her. I'm not trying to make her uncomfortable, she's just really fucking pretty.

The drive back to the shop is quick, and she doesn't say much, just looks out the window, her arms folded across her stomach. When we get to the shop, I send her inside while I unload the car into our lot. I'd like to have her stay outside with me, but it's hot and I'm trying not to be a jerk.

When I walk back into the shop, she's not in the waiting area where I'm expecting her to be. I grab two bottles of water out of the cooler and go looking for her.

9

PARKER

I wander through the auto shop, searching for the bathroom. I open a door, but it's just an office. No dice. I'm about to close the door when I see the Juniper Kerry novel sitting on the desk. It's the same one I gave Lukas all of four days ago, but it's almost unrecognizable from the shiny, crisp novel I shoved into his chest as I pushed him out the door.

I pick it up, bewildered at the condition. The pages are dog-eared, and it looks as though it's been through at least one water balloon fight. The whole dang book is rippled with water damage, there are grease stains all over the place, the cover is torn up on one side and there's a chunk missing off one corner.

A throat clears behind me, startling me and making me jump. I turn to face Lukas, feeling guilty for snooping in his office. His coveralls are folded down around his waist, his broad chest wrapped in a grease-stained white t-shirt. There's still a black grease streak on his cheekbone, but it only makes him look more handsome. The tattoos on his arms are visible and God, am I a sucker for those things.

Refusing to give him the satisfaction of gawking at him, I hold up the paperback. "Are you a monster?"

Lukas grins at me as he steps into the office, "Careful, I'm not done with that." He reaches out to take the book, his fingers brushing mine as I release it. I'm suddenly aware of how very small this office is. Lukas is wearing a lazy smirk as he runs a hand over the book like he has a secret he's not sharing with the room.

"Careful?" I laugh. "That thing looks like it's been through a woodchipper. How on earth did you do that much damage in four days?" I ask, curious if a little horrified.

"I was reading it out back and set it down on the table. Asher accidentally got it with the hose." He points at the gouged corner. "That was a slip with the drill." He rubs a hand over the cover, "And this was where Jack backed over it on his bike."

I watch his fingers caress the cover and the worst part of me wants him to run those fingers over my neck and across my chest. I weirdly love the idea that he was carrying it around the garage with him, reading it in his free time.

"So, you read it? Are reading it, I mean?"

Lukas looks at me, eyebrows drawn down like he thinks I'm being a little crazy. "Yeah."

"Why?"

"What do you mean, why? Because it's good. What's with the third degree? You're the one who gave it to me, Parker."

"Yeah, but...I thought you were just making fun of me. Never mind. I'm glad you like it. There are like five more in the series," I say awkwardly. I don't know where to look, so I settle on the book in his grease-stained hands. Fudgesicles. Why is that turning me on?

"I should call for a ride," I blurt, pulling out my phone. I can't really afford a Lyft, but I don't have any other options until I figure out how to pay for my car repairs. I flinch as I remember that all of this is going to be catastrophically expensive.

"Um, I know this is weird because she's your sister and it's not like she works here, but Lilah said I could do a payment plan or something," I say, staring at the phone in my hands.

"We'll figure it out. Don't worry about the cost right now," Lukas says. I get the impression he's being cagey, but I'm not sure why.

"Okay... thanks." I edge around him towards the door, playing with my phone. "I'll just wait outside until my ride gets here." I'm opening the rideshare app when Lukas puts a hand on my elbow, holding me next to him. That small touch, his calloused hand on my skin, makes me burn.

"I'll give you a ride home."

"No," I say too quickly, too loudly. "I mean, no thank you. I already owe you more than I can repay right now. I don't want to waste the rest of your Saturday. I'll call for a ride."

"But I'd like to give you a ride."

Oh my. Why did he have to word it like that? I'm picturing a very different kind of ride than the one he's offering. He's so close I can feel the heat from his chest on my shoulder, his breath teasing my skin. The heady combination of his closeness and the innuendo buried in his offer sends a blush spreading across my face and my breath catching in my chest. It's probably too much to hope that he missed my reaction.

Lukas smiles at me, and it's not his usual smirk. It's softer, sweeter. And the way his eyes search mine is so… intimate. Why does he make me feel like this? Like I know him so much better than I do. It defies every interaction I've had with him.

"Come on, I'm heading out anyway. Besides, it's not like I had big plans tonight."

Right. So I'm only a minor inconvenience. I release a lungful of air and it comes out more of a huff than I meant it to, but Lukas is being nice. I know he's not into me, but we could be friendly, right? I mean, I'm close with his sisters. It's not like either of us is going anywhere. And maybe I'm just a glutton for punishment, but it's impossible to turn down a little more time with him.

"Yeah, okay. Thank you."

Lukas' smile pulls up higher on one side. "Great. Do you mind hanging out for a second? Asher should have closed everything up, but I need to double-check."

I nod. "Sure." I take the book from his hands and drop into one of the chairs facing his desk. Lukas chuckles with an actual full smile as he steps out. I look at the book, shaking my head at the dog-eared pages before picking a spot in the middle.

"Monster," I whisper as I see the writing in the margin. *Ask Parker*

43

about the tusks is scrawled next to a description of one of the alien races. He underlined one of the sex scenes with a note that reads *Parker is a dirty bird* and it makes me laugh. I flip through the rest of the novel looking for notes and laughing at his comments. A little knock on the door frame rips me back to reality and I look up, my mouth still curved in a smile.

"You ready?" he asks.

"Found your notes," I say with a raised eyebrow. He reaches out and takes the book back, setting it on the desk, a little pink tinging his cheeks. It's then that I realize he's cleaned the grease from his face. His hands are clean, and he's changed into fresh clothes too. The white t-shirt is stretched over his chest and arms, and it's all I can do to keep my hands to myself.

"Forgot about those," he says, offering a hand to help me up. He keeps doing that. I almost don't dare touch his hand. The way his touch affects me is… intense. But I suck it up and take his hand, letting him pull me to my feet. He holds my hand in his big calloused one as he leads me out of the office. He stops at a closet by the front door and grabs a leather jacket, putting it over my shoulders.

"I'm not cold," I say, baffled.

"I know," he says with a little smile. "Trust me." I shrug but put my arms in the sleeves, trying to ignore the fact that it smells like him. A hint of cologne and engine oil and leather. Lukas zips me up and grabs a helmet from the closet. A motorcycle helmet.

"Wait, are you driving me home on your motorcycle?" I ask. I guess the answer is obvious, but I'm more than a little panicked at the thought. "I've never even sat on one. What if I fall off?"

Lukas chuckles. "You won't fall off. Just hold on tight and lean with me," he says, putting the helmet on my head and adjusting the strap under my chin. I feel like a child, a parent buckling me in to go play on a bike. Not that my parents did that kind of stuff. They bought me a helmet and told me to figure it out.

He grabs a helmet and puts it on before leading me outside. His motorcycle is parked right out front and it is *huge* up close; all black and shiny chrome. He grabs the handles and kicks a leg over the seat, effortlessly settling in. He pats the black leather seat behind him. It's tiny. I can't sit there. I'll be plastered to his back the entire way home. I look at it, then back at Lukas and I'm sure the alarm is written all over my face.

"I- I should just call for a ride," I tell him.

Lukas' mouth pulls to the side, his green eyes serious as he holds out his hand. "Come on, Freckles. Just trust me."

I eye his hand and weigh my options. Chicken out and pay for a ride or grow a pair and wrap myself around Lukas like a baby monkey.

"I'm not sure I want to ride in the bitch seat," I say.

His serious expression cracks and he shakes his head at me. "No one calls it that outside of Sons of Anarchy."

"Oh, yes, they do!" I argue. "And I'm not getting on there if it's going to make me club sweetbutt."

Lukas leans over the handlebars, laughing so hard he's shaking the bike.

"Sweetbutt? You're hilarious, but you might need to take a break on the motorcycle romances. Get on. I promise not to pass you around or let anyone say you're riding bitch."

I wanted to be more spontaneous, right? What's more spontaneous than hopping on the back of a hot man's motorcycle? And as terrifying as the motorcycle looks, New Parker isn't a pussy.

I can do this.

I put my hand in his and throw my right leg over the back of the seat. I'm nowhere nearly as graceful as Lukas was, but I get up behind him and wiggle until I'm centered on the seat. My hands are on his shoulders, my grip light as I lean backward, trying to create a little space between us. His muscles bunch under my fingertips as he chuckles and reaches back, grabbing my wrists one by one, and wrapping my arms around his middle.

"Hold on tight," he says, his voice muffled by the helmet. His thumb strokes the back of my hand before he lets go and grips the handle. "Keep your feet up on the pegs and don't put your leg against the exhaust," he says. I glance down to check the position of the big chrome exhaust pipe.

"Okay," I reply shakily.

"Just tap my shoulder if you hate it. I'll pull over and we'll get you a car. Ready?"

I nod before I realize he can't see me. "Yes?" I answer. I feel the chuckle in his chest and I'm pressed so close that it vibrates through me. My nipples tighten in response to him and I'm insanely grateful for his big leather jacket, even if it is miserably hot because it's the only thing hiding the way he's affecting me.

Lukas' muscles flex as the bike roars to life, vibrating underneath us as he revs the engine. A thrilling tingle runs through me as we roll forward. Lukas speeds up gently and we pull out of the parking lot, hitting the main road. We pick up speed and the wind blows over us and even in the leather, it feels amazing. I'm still clutching my arms around him, but I relax a little as I realize how easy it is to just hang on. It's not as wobbly as I expected, and Lukas is so confident and solid. I can't say that I mind being wrapped around him like this.

"How are you doing back there, Freckles?" Lukas asks as we stop at a red light.

"Good!" I tell him honestly. "This is fun!" He puts a hand over mine for just a second. It feels like a tiny acknowledgment that he likes this too.

"You're from Minnesota, right?" he asks.

"Yeah, all the way up North." There's no point in telling him the name of my town. I guarantee he's never heard of Middle River. At last count, we had a population of 312. I guess 311 now that I'm gone. I wonder if Daniel Jones got up on his ladder and painted over the "2" with a "1," or if they decided to just leave it. "Downtown" Middle River takes up a grand total of two blocks. We have one bar, one diner, one school building, and zero stoplights.

"That's a big change." He chuckles. "How do you like being so near to the beach?" he asks. We've reached the other side of town and the wind picks up as our speed increases.

"I've never been," I yell back.

He tosses a look over his shoulder at me as the light turns green. We only ride a couple hundred feet before he pulls over on the side of the road.

"What's wrong?" I ask. I don't think I can handle two breakdowns in one day.

Lukas takes off his helmet, turning so he can look at me fully, his bright green eyes searching mine. "What do you mean you've never been?"

"To the beach? I mean I've never been. I drove straight to Sonoma when I moved here and haven't been any farther West than that." That's pretty self-explanatory, right?

"But you never went as a kid? Even out East?"

I shake my head. "We went to a lake once, but my dad is a pastor and my mom is a librarian. They didn't exactly have the funds to run off on beach vacations anytime they wanted."

Not that they would have, even if we'd had the money, I add silently because I've already admitted enough.

Lukas' eyes are piercing as he looks at me. They narrow slightly and he scowls before putting his helmet back on. I tighten my grip around him as we move again, but Lukas checks the traffic and does a U-turn, heading back through town.

"What are you doing now?" I ask, poking his side gently.

"We're going to the beach," he replies, his voice firm.

"I can't. I have work to do at home!" I argue.

"It can't wait until tomorrow?" he asks. I want to argue, even open my mouth to tell him that no, it can't wait, but that's not true. I was just going to put on pajamas and go to bed early like a grandma.

"That's what I thought," he chuckles. "I'm kidnapping you."

I'm not sure how we've gone from taunting and yelling at each other in a bar to *this* in 24 hours. We hit the highway, and it's too loud to talk, but I love the feel of the wind rushing around us. I relax into Lukas' back, adjusting my grip so that my palms are flat on his chest instead of clutching my own forearms. There's an inch of tattoo peeking out the back of his shirt and climbing up his neck. The tip of a bird's wing, I think. The feathers are exquisitely detailed and I have the strongest urge to press my lips to it.

I love the way he feels. He's warm and solid, and I'm hyper-aware of my thighs straddling his hips. I scold myself for being turned on by it. He's being nice to me, but that doesn't mean anything. He's just unwittingly fulfilling my favorite fantasy, and my vivid imagination is happy to fill in the rest.

10

LUKAS

I know the drive out to Point Reyes like the back of my hand. It's only forty-five minutes of quiet highway, but I could ride all night with Parker's warm body pressed to my back. After a couple minutes, I feel her relax against me, her soft hands pressing into my skin through my shirt. The real challenge is ignoring the way her legs feel wrapped around me.

The sun is low in the sky when we reach the parking lot. Parker loosens her grip on me and I hold her hand, helping her off the bike behind me. There's excitement in her wide eyes as she waits for me to dismount. She stretches and smiles at me as she removes my jacket and the spare helmet. The wind makes her hair flutter around her face and I can smell the ocean on the salty breeze as I lead her down the trail.

Kehoe Beach is a half-mile walk through boardwalk trails and sand dunes, and Parker is fascinated by every little thing we pass. The little birds skipping through the dunes make her laugh out loud and the sound grips my chest. When we crest the last dune and the shore comes into view she gasps, stopping in her tracks. Her hand goes to her mouth as she takes in the waves crash on the wide sandy beach. Little sandpipers chase the water as it retreats, running from each fresh surge. Parker's gaze sweeps up the shore to the rocky cliffs in the distance.

And I can't take my eyes off her.

When she looks back at me, her hair blows around her and she looks as if she's a mermaid emerging from the deep—a siren calling to a sailor, urging him into the waves. I've never seen anything so beautiful. I can't breathe but I'd go anywhere she beckoned. I want to memorize the line of her jaw, the curve of her lips, and the wide-eyed overwhelmed joy in her expression.

"Thank you," she whispers.

Those words squeeze my chest and something in my soul rearranges, tying me to this moment forever. I don't know what to say, so I just nod as she looks back out at the sea, my heart stuttering as I watch her. The wind blows her hair back, whipping it around her face and shoulders as she takes a long, deep breath.

I could watch Parker gaze out at the ocean like this forever but all too soon, she glances back, beaming at me, eyes bright as she grabs my elbow for balance and hops around, yanking off her sneakers. I do my best to steady her while still holding our helmets. She tucks her socks into her shoes and takes off running down the sand dunes to the water. Sandpipers and seagulls scatter as she gets near the water.

"Wait!" I call out. "It's c—"

Her feet hit the water, and she screams, turning and running back up the beach as I laugh.

"It's cold!" I yell out to her as I struggle out of my boots.

"No crap!" she yells back, laughing. Setting our stuff in the sand, I wrap my jacket around the helmets to keep sand out of the padding and join her at the edge of the surf. Parker digs her toes into the wet sand, watching the little air bubbles that pop up all around us.

"What are those?" she asks.

"Little clams, mostly," I tell her.

"That's wild," she says, holding her hair over one shoulder while she bends down to look at them. Her ass is inches from my fingers and it's all I can do not to run my hand over those denim curves. I can't take my eyes off her hips and the way her waist nips in above them.

The way she's bent over is filling my mind with the dirtiest thoughts, and it's all I can do not to groan out loud.

I wouldn't press my luck with her, though. I got her to come out here with me, and that should be enough for now. And as much as I want to rip her clothes off and taste every inch of her, I don't want to rush this. I want to savor my time with her.

I'm so distracted by watching Parker (and thinking dirty thoughts about her) that I miss the rogue wave heading our way until it's too late. The freezing water hits my knees, so cold it feels like million pins pricking my shins and feet.

"Shit," I yelp, hopping in place like that's going to help.

Parker lets out a little scream as she loses her balance and falls face-first towards the foamy water. Without thinking, I shoot out a hand, grabbing hold of her shirt and hauling her back against me as the water rushes back out to sea around our feet. I scoop her up and move up the beach, safe from the frigid water.

Parker has an arm around my neck, her other hand on my chest as she looks up at me with wide eyes. Her pretty lips are parted in a little 'O', her breathing shallow as I set her on her feet in the warm sand, my hand on her elbow. Her hands rest on my chest for barely a second before she pulls back, blushing.

"Thank you," she says breathlessly. "That was crazy."

"Anytime, Freckles."

I sit in the dry sand, pulling Parker down next to me. She isn't touching me but she's close enough that I can sense her body near mine.

We sit in companionable silence, watching the sandpipers run along the foamy surf and the pelicans bob on the waves as the sun sets.

"I can't believe you've never been to the beach before," I say after a while.

Parker is running her fingers through the sand, a little collection of shells piled next to her knee.

"Yeah, well... my parents weren't exactly the fun, family vacation type. I told you we went to a lake once. That was only because my parents had to fumigate the house and the cabin at the lake was close and cheap."

"Jesus, that sucks. My gran brought us out to the beach all the time as kids. I don't think a week went by in any given summer that we weren't out here. When I was a teenager, my friends and I used to sneak out to a secluded beach up north to drink and party." The smell of beer still reminds me of sitting in the sand, the smell of salty air mixing with the smoke from a bonfire…

"I don't have many memories of my mother, but I remember her bringing me here the summer before she died. She loved Kehoe Beach, especially the cliffs." I say, gesturing up the shoreline.

Parker gives me a sweet, sad smile. "Your sisters told me about your parents. I'm so sorry." She watches me for a second with those round blue eyes. "It sounds like your gran gave you a great childhood though."

"Yeah, and I gave her the last of those gray hairs in return," I laugh.

Parker snorts. "Yeah, I've heard about that too. Did you really get stuck on top of the water tower?"

"Okay, to be fair, I was fourteen. I did it on a dare and I don't love heights. And when I got up there, the top rung of the ladder was rusted and broke right out from under my foot."

"Holy crap! You could have died," Parker says, smacking me on the arm and frowning.

I shake my head, laughing. "I know. It was awful. I was stuck for hours until the fire department got someone up there to help me down. Gran was *livid.*"

Parker laughs. "Yeah, I can imagine. I'm surprised she didn't lock you up and throw away the key."

The sky is burning orange and pink over the water, casting a warm glow over Parker's face and lighting her hair a bright coppery color as she grins at me. I smile back as she turns her gaze back out to the waves. I want to touch her. I want to feel every inch of her skin under my hands. I want to trace her freckles with my lips.

"So, why Sonoma?" I ask her. She hesitates, keeping her eyes straight ahead as she answers.

"I just… found the shop for rent online. It was my chance to get out of Middle River and away from my parents."

"I take it you're not close," I say.

Parker scoffs. "No. We have a difference of opinion on just about everything."

"Like what?"

"Like my father is a bible thumper and my mother is a librarian who despises romance novels. She caught me with one when I was fifteen and burned it. Literally. She threw it in the fireplace. Then they locked me in my room for a week. They insisted on homeschooling me, even though neither of them liked me very much. They just didn't want me interacting with "those sinful public-school kids.""

She says the last part in a grumpy man's voice, shaking her head at the memory, and my stomach turns at the thought of living with someone like that. Then again, I'm probably lucky I don't remember much about my own dad.

"I just couldn't live like that anymore," she says.

"I don't blame you," I say, watching her face and the sad little frown on her lips.

"I wanted a fresh start, you know. I wanted to be someone new. Someone spontaneous and brave."

"Is that what this is? Why you got on the bike?" I ask her, watching her eyes as she follows the sandpipers running from the surf. "Is that part of the brave new you? Because if it is, I like it." I bump her shoulder with mine, trying to lighten the mood.

"Why are you being so nice to me today?" Parker asks, catching me off guard. She keeps her face turned out toward the water, refusing to look at me.

"What do you mean?" I ask.

"Are you being obtuse on purpose?" she asks, wrinkling her brow.

I can't help laughing at that. "No. I just… I like you. I like being near you."

"Oh, clearly," she scoffs. "You tell your sisters I'm not your type, you come to my bookshop just to make fun of me, you call me names, and the bar…"

"Hold up, I never said I'm a nice guy but didn't go to your shop to make fun of you and I don't call you names," I say defensively. It's true that I've been a bit of an ass, but I'm not a complete dick.

She glares up at me and points at her own face. "Freckles?"

I'm shocked and my mouth hangs open as I realize what she's saying. She thought I was making fun of her? Really? I lean closer, my nose just a couple of inches from hers, and look her in the eyes as I quietly tell her, "That's a nickname. I *like* your freckles. I went to your bookstore because I wanted to see you."

Parker's eyes are enormous as they search mine. "I *heard* you tell Lilah I'm not your type," she says, her voice achingly soft. I wish she'd never hear that.

"I lied," I say.

Parker frowns slightly, her lips pouty and her eyebrows scrunched up. "Why?"

"Why? Because I wanted Lilah off my ass. I didn't even know you were there."

Parker glances down at her feet, buried in the sand. I hate that I hurt her. I hate the way I acted at the bar last night, and I hate more than anything that she thought I was mocking her. She deserves so much better than that. If self-loathing was an Olympic sport, I'd be on the pedestal with a goddamn gold medal right now.

11

PARKER

I want to believe him. I really do.

Maybe he wasn't trying to make fun of me with the freckles thing. And I can see how maybe I misconstrued that whole bookstore encounter… but he was such a douche last night at Sally's party. He can't possibly expect me to be ok with the things he said.

"Ok, but the bar. What the hell was that?"

Lukas gives me a thoughtful look, his eyes searching my face. He takes a lock of my hair and curls it around his finger, playing with it as he leans closer.

"I was being an ass."

"Why?" I whisper.

His lips brush my cheek, his beard tickles my jaw, coarse but softer than I expected. I close my eyes and lean toward him, unable to fight the pull I feel. I swear, I lose control of my muscles around this man. It's a miracle I can keep my hands in the sand; the last vestige of neutral territory.

"Because I was mad. At him. At you. I couldn't stand him looking at you like that. But Parker… no matter what I feel, you shouldn't want me. You should be with someone better. I tried to fight this. I really did. You just… you make me crazy."

His fingertips stroke along my jaw as he presses kisses along my cheek. At his touch, tingles dance through my body, every cell in my being reacting to him. I don't pull away even though part of me, the rational, boring, self-preserving side of me, is screaming to run for the hills. This man is going to break my heart, but I don't think I can stop myself.

Lukas lifts my chin with his fingers and thumb, pulling back to look at me. I'm frozen as those deep green eyes, filled with burning intensity, hold me.

He leans close, grazing his lips over mine, so gently I feel the electricity between us more than the physical touch. He kisses me again, pulling my bottom lip between his. My breath catches in my chest and I hesitate for a second before New Parker takes over, leaping fearlessly into the dark.

I grab a fistful of his shirt and kiss him back. A pleased, relieved sort of groan vibrates through Lukas' chest as he teases my lip with his tongue. My lips part and his tongue sweeps into my mouth, tangling with mine. He cups my jaw, holding me close. His free hand winds around my back, his fingertips pressing into my lower back as he drags me closer in the sand.

Lukas winds his fingers through my hair while his warm hand slides over my hip and down my leg, the touch somewhere between reverent and possessive. I moan, but the sound is caught in our kiss. His fingers feel so good gripping my thigh like that. Desire like I've never experienced before washes through me, hot and itchy, and it makes me tremble.

Lukas pulls back, breaking the kiss and regarding me with hunger in his eyes.

"Is this okay?" he asks.

"Oh, yeah," I reply breathlessly, pulling him close and kissing him again. I feel his smile against my lips as he pulls my thigh over his legs. I go happily, straddling him, my knees pressed into the warm sand as my chest presses against his. I wrap my arms around his neck, enjoying the solid feel of him underneath me. Lukas buries a hand in my hair as he pulls me closer, his arm around my back like an iron bar, holding me tight. He's so big. I feel enveloped by him. Protected.

His hand in my hair tightens, holding me in place, and the sensation sends tingles down my spine. Lukas slides his other hand up under the back of my shirt. His work-roughened hands roam over my skin, caressing my spine and dragging over my ribs. He moves slowly, every touch an exploration. He cups my breast, his thumb dragging over my nipple, and even through the fabric of my bra, it feels incredible.

Need spirals up through me, quick and demanding. A moan rips its way out of my throat as I feel his hard length trapped between us. Even with the layers of clothing, his erection is hot and hard under me. When I rock against him, he growls at the friction and bites my lip gently. I wonder if he has any idea how wet I am.

My heart races at the thought of him slipping a hand inside my jeans and touching me. Oh God, I need him to slow down. Or maybe speed up? Either way, I want to rip his clothes off and feel every inch of his skin against mine. I want to run my fingers over his tattoos. I'm frantic to get closer, single-minded in my desperate need for more. I grind my hips down on him, pleasure spreading through me even as it makes the need grow bigger.

"Lukas," I pant his name. I want more. I want everything.

"Parker," Lukas says hoarsely, and it's a tortured, breathless sound. He pulls my hair back, exposing my neck, and kisses his way down the column of my throat. His teeth scrape my skin, sending a shiver through my body. Lukas nips the sensitive skin at the juncture of my neck and collarbone, eliciting a moan and a fresh wave of moisture in my panties.

"Fuck," he mutters as his hands grab my hips, holding them still. "You can't keep that up, Parker. You're going to make me embarrass myself."

A little thrill runs through me as I realize what he's saying. The thought that I could make him lose control makes me feel powerful, and now there's nothing in this world I want more.

"Don't smirk at me like that," he says as his fingertips grip my hips. There's a hint of teasing in his tone, but it's buried under layers of growly command that, oddly enough, are doing nothing to encourage me to stop.

"So, how long do I have to sit still for?" I tease him, looking down at the sand with a smile.

Lukas winds his fingers through my hair, gripping it and angling my face back towards his.

"That depends. How long can I convince you to stay there?"

12

LUKAS

Parker wets her lips and smiles at me. There's a hazy, sultry edge to the way she's looking at me that I never expected. Under that sweet shell, she's all fire and I think I'd happily let her burn me alive.

I'm still hard as hell, turned on to the point of being painful, and every tiny move she makes on my lap is equal parts pleasure and torture. I'd kill to strip her bare and sink myself deep inside her, but she deserves better than that. Jesus, she deserves so much better than me, but hell if I can let her go.

Releasing her hair, I run my fingers down her neck and kiss her. I can feel her pulse racing under my fingertips as she kisses me back with soft little sighs. We've got to get out of here or I'm going to fuck this up.

I ease off, even though it fucking kills me. "Come on. I'm getting you some dinner."

"Now?"

"Yes, now."

"But… you're still kind of…" She looks down between us and blushes.

I raise my eyebrows at her shy expression. She was grinding on my lap like two minutes ago, but now she's shy?

"I'll be fine. And you have to let me buy you dinner. I kidnapped you. Those are the rules."

"I didn't realize there were rules for this kind of thing," Parker laughs as she slides off my lap onto the sand beside me. The rasp of her movement sets my dick aching all over again and I groan, drawing my legs up and taking a deep breath. *I can do this. I can wait. Nobody wants sand in their ass.* Parker gives me a sympathetic look, but there's a smug edge to it she can't hide.

Sighing, I stand and hold my hand out to her. She takes it with a smile and lets me pull her to her feet.

"Let's go, Freckles."

Parker takes one last look out at the ocean. "Fine, but I'm coming back as soon as you fix my car."

I want to tell her not to hold her breath. The Civic is beyond fixing, but I don't want to upset her or make her worry about it right now.

"Or I could drive you out again sometime," I tell her as I take her hand and tug her up towards the walkway and our helmets.

She gives me a smile, but it doesn't reach her eyes.

We shake off as much sand as we can and put our shoes back on. The sun drops below the horizon as we walk back to my bike, and it takes longer to wind our way back.

"Where are we going to eat?" Parker asks. "We're a mess."

She's not wrong. We're both salty and damp from the knees down, windblown and dusty from the sand.

"I know a place," I tell her.

"Very mysterious," she teases.

I laugh as I put the helmet on her head, securing the straps before wrapping her back up in my leather jacket.

I get on the bike and pat the seat for her to hop on. She doesn't hesitate this time. Her warm little hand grips my shoulder as she throws a leg over the back and shimmies into place before wrapping her arms around my waist. I reach back and squeeze her thigh. She feels so… right. I can't pin it down, but I love the feel of her behind me like this. I've taken girls for rides before, but it was always more stressful than anything else.

"Ready?" I ask.

"Yes, sir," she teases. I suppress the growl of pleasure that little phrase stirs in me. She has no clue how fucking sexy she is.

I rev the engine before pulling out of the parking lot. We fly down the little two-lane highway until I see the string lights and the bright pink taco truck. I pull into the gravel lot and kill the engine. Parker holds onto my bicep as she climbs off the back and grins at me as she undoes the helmet.

"Tacos," she sighs happily.

I run a hand through my hair. Maybe I should have taken her somewhere nicer. This was just the first thing I thought of, but now what we're here I'm realizing I could have done better. I mean, these are the best tacos for a hundred miles, but Parker deserves more than dinner on the side of the road. "Yeah, It's not exactly white tablecloths—"

"It's perfect," she interrupts me with a hand on my chest and a sweet smile. God, the look on her face. She's practically glowing. You'd think I took her to The French Laundry instead of Anita's Taco Stand. But I'm realizing I may have misjudged a lot of things about Parker.

Anita, the owner of the taco stand, has been running it since I was a kid. She's also friends with my gran, something I didn't consider until just now. She gives me a raised eyebrow as Parker and I approach the window. Parker's too busy reading the menu to catch the look, but I sure do. I'd bet my left nut she'll be texting my gran five seconds after we leave.

"Hi Anita," I say as I lean against the truck, trying to lay on the charm.

"Hi yourself," she replies. "You staying out of trouble?" she asks, making me chuckle. Ten years on the straight and narrow and she still always asks me the same thing.

"Mostly," I answer back.

She purses her lips and squints at me like she doesn't quite believe me. "Mm-hm," she says before turning her attention to Parker. "Hey sweetie, what can I getcha?"

"One taco al pastor and one shredded pork, please," Parker says with a smile.

"That's it? That's not enough!" Anita teases. "They're little. You need at least three."

Parker blushes. "Oh, um… that's ok. I had a big lunch, but thank you." She reaches into her purse, digging for her wallet, but I put my hand on her arm. I know she's worried about money. I've heard enough from my sisters, even before her car exploded, to know that she's barely getting by. Something I'm going to find a way to fix.

"I've got you, Freckles," I say before adding six tacos, two ears of grilled corn, and two cups of homemade lemonade to the order. She tries to argue, but I shut her down with a quick kiss as I hand my credit card to Anita. "Kidnapper pays, those are the rules," I say.

She laughs and gives up, but Anita gives me a suspicious look as she hands my card back, spinning the iPad around for me to sign.

"You kidnapped her? Should I be calling the police?" She asks, looking Parker up and down. "She looks too young for you. You're not robbing the cradle, are you Lukas?" Parker blushes bright red and stutters as I laugh.

"No ma'am," I say. "She's a willing victim. Mostly."

Parker finds her voice, "It's true. He took me to the beach, and I swear, I'm older than I look."

Anita smiles at that. "Oh, I'm just teasing sweetie. Lukas is a good man. Just mind he treats you like a lady because—"

"Thanks, Anita!" I interrupt before she can tell Parker any horror stories from my youth. Anita knows way too much.

Her summer help, a frazzled-looking teenager, hands me a tray loaded with food. He slides the lemonade towards us. Parker picks them up with a quiet "Thank you" and a smile that makes the kid blush. I can't say I blame him, but I stare him down, anyway. Placing my free hand on the small of her back, I lead her to a picnic table at the far corner of the gravel lot.

I sit next to Parker and hand her one of the al pastor tacos. She takes a big bite and moans as she chews it. The sound goes straight to my dick. I can just imagine her moaning like that as I sink inside her—

"Why are you watching me eat?" she asks, interrupting a fantasy that was getting dirtier by the second.

"You're sexy as hell," I say.

She laughs like she doesn't believe me, looking back down at the tray and changing the subject.

"I don't know how you're going to eat all that."

"I'm not," I say. "You're going to help. I know for a fact you haven't eaten anything in hours."

Right on cue, her stomach rumbles.

I give her an I-told-you-so face, holding an ear of corn out for her. She rolls her eyes but takes it with a smile. We eat happily, conversation on hold until the tray in front of us is all taco wrappers and empty salsa containers.

"God, that was so good," Parker sighs before sipping on her lemonade.

"Best tacos in California," I tell her. I want to sit here all night. I know I'm going to have to take her home but I'm not ready to let her go yet. I want more of her. The little touches, the sweet smiles... all of it.

The universe seems to be working against me, though. Lightning flashes and thunder rumbles from the direction of the beach. Fuck. I don't want Parker riding on my bike in a storm. Besides being dangerous, it just sucks to ride through anything more than a drizzle.

"Time to go, Freckles. We should get you home."

Parker nods, but I'm gratified to see she doesn't look happy either. We wave goodbye to Anita who blows a kiss at Parker before pointing two fingers at her eyes and then me in the universal gesture for *I'm-watching-you-so-don't-fuck-it-up.*

I give Anita a salute in return and turn back towards Parker. She tucks her hands in her back pockets as we walk and I rest my hand on her lower back, rubbing my fingers along the waistband of her jeans. Parker looks down at the gravel, a smile spreading across her face.

"What are you grinning at?" I ask her.

"Nothing," Parker answers too quickly. Even in the dim light, I can see her cheeks pink up.

"Uh-huh, looks like nothing," I tease her. I'd pay a million bucks to know what was going on in her brain right now.

"I, uh… I like Anita," Parker fumbles as we reach the bike.

"Everyone likes Anita," I say as I put my jacket around her shoulders. I'm starting to like the way she looks in it. "You should meet her wife, Josie. She's wild. They went to Vegas with Gran and Sally a couple of years ago. They got carried away and their weekend turned into a week, comped, at the Cosmopolitan."

Parker laughs, "You're joking."

I shake my head and grin at her. "Nope, they all got matching tattoos, too."

"The dice on Sally's wrist?"

I nod. "Gran got hers on an ankle, Anita's is on her shoulder, and I haven't seen it, but apparently Josie got a tramp stamp." Parker cackles, head thrown back.

"God, I couldn't keep up with them."

"No one can," I reply. "Or at least, no one should."

Lightning keeps flashing in the distance, not so close that we're in danger, but I can smell rain in the air. I hurry us onto the bike and we pull out of the lot, gravel crunching under the tires. Parker holds on tight as headlights fly by us.

We're still five miles from town when the skies open up; cold, heavy rain falling in sheets. The summer heat doesn't last more than a couple of minutes in the deluge. We're soaked through by the time we hit Main Street and I can feel Parker shivering behind me, her helmet tucked down behind my shoulder.

"How far out do you live?" I shout back at her.

"Fifteen minutes," she yells, gesturing to the east side of town. I put a hand on her thigh, resting behind mine. The soaking wet denim is chilled, and she gives another racking shiver.

"Nope. Not happening," I mutter. No way in hell I'm going to keep her on the bike for another fifteen minutes, shivering like that. That, and I'm not willing to risk laying down my bike on wet pavement with Parker on the back.

I swing to the left and head towards my house.

She smacks my thigh. "You can't keep kidnapping me!" she yells over the wind and rain pelting our helmets, but I just shrug. From where I'm sitting, it looks like I'm going to get away with it. I should feel guilty, but I don't. And I should be miserable, all cold and wet like this but the way Parker's pressed against me, her thighs spread around my hips, arms wrapped around my waist, a hand on my stomach and a palm on my chest, I feel like a goddamn king.

13

PARKER

I want to be annoyed that he's not taking me home, but as long as there's a warm change of clothes, I'm here for it. I melt into his back as I shiver behind him on the bike. I know his broad shoulders and chest are blocking the worst of the wind and rain. He must be miserable, taking the brunt of the storm for me like that.

We drive down a quiet street to a little house, just a minute or two from downtown. Lukas pulls into the driveway and under the garage door as it's still opening and parks next to a big black pickup truck.

Water drips from my shaking hand as I grip Lukas' bicep, dismounting. Even rain-soaked and freezing, it makes me happy to think I'm getting better at this. I don't love the whole rain thing but otherwise, I could really get used to riding with him, as long as no one says I'm riding bitch. And with Lukas glaring at them, I'm sure no one would dare.

Lukas follows me off the bike and my breath catches at the sight of him. If I thought I was soaked, it's nothing compared to him. His white t-shirt is plastered to his front and I can see the tattoos across his chest, distorted through the dripping wet fabric. His jeans cling to his thick thighs and all I can think about is how it felt to straddle those thighs on the beach.

The garage door shuts behind us as we drip on the concrete floor, staring at each other until I shiver again. Lukas shakes his head as if clearing it and holds out his hand to me.

"Come on, let's get you warmed up."

I hesitate because I'm not sure where this is going, and that's kind of exhilarating. Old Parker wouldn't go home with a man under any circumstances. But what am I going to do? Stand out here shivering all night? I'd much rather see where the night goes with Lukas. So I take the offered hand and try not to smile at the way my hand tucks into his so perfectly.

Lukas leads me through a door to a kitchen, and it is *freezing* inside. It would probably feel great if I'd walked in during the heat of the day in dry clothes. But soaked through and already chilled, it feels like torture. I'm covered with goosebumps and shivering violently.

He pulls me along so quickly that I just catch glimpses of things. Pots and pans hanging over an island cooktop. Granite counters atop modern cabinets. Everything is clean, save a pizza box sticking way out of the trash. I laugh as he leads me through the dining room and towards a living area with big leather couches. A massive TV is hung over the fireplace, shelves full of books on either side.

"What are you laughing at, Freckles?" Lukas asks.

"I don't know. I guess it's just not what I expected."

He chuckles. "You mean it's not a biker clubhouse? Nobody's getting a tattoo in the corner?"

I stutter, trying to come up with a response as he leads me upstairs. "Well, I mean— It's just so clean."

Lukas smirks back at me. "Sorry to disappoint you. I'll rough it up for you next time."

Pulling back on his hand, I make him turn to look at me. "Hey. Th-that's not what I meant. I'm not disappointed. Thank you for bringing me here."

Lukas looks me up and down, rubbing his hand along his jaw. His smile is soft, but his eyes are hungry and it makes me want more than just a place to warm up. "Yeah, well, I couldn't let you get hypother-mia, now could I?"

I shake my head slowly, watching his lips as he talks, mesmerized.

Lukas pulls me down the hall to the master bedroom and into the bathroom. A glass shower dominates the back half of it. I drop my purse on the edge of the sink as he pulls a towel out of a cabinet and hands it to me.

"Alright, here's a towel. Shampoo's in the shower..." Lukas says as he backs toward the door, running his hand through his hair. "The water gets really hot, so be careful."

He's leaving, I realize. Well, that's disappointing. I don't know what I expected, but it sure as hell wasn't that. I don't want him to go. I'm New Parker, dammit! I made out with a man on the beach today. I rode on a motorcycle!

"Where are you going?" I ask quietly. Lukas' hands are clenched by his sides, the muscles in his arms tight. His jaw twitches as he looks back at me. His rain-soaked jeans cling to his skin, and I can't help noticing the bulge straining the front of his pants. It sure doesn't look like he wants to leave.

"Guest shower," he grunts, gesturing his head back down the hallway. I fiddle with the bottom of my tank top as he turns to leave. I'm a chicken at heart, but New Parker isn't having any of it.

"Or you could stay," I call after him.

Lukas reappears almost instantly, leaning in the doorframe.

"Is that what you want, Freckles?" he asks. His voice is low, and he's smoldering so hard I'm surprised my ovaries don't burst into flames. "Be sure. Because if I come in there, I'm not going to be able to keep my hands off you."

Yes. Yes, that is definitely what I want. But words are failing me, and if I try to talk, I'm afraid I'll just squeak. Trying to be braver than I feel, I look him right in those stunning green eyes, drop the towel on the floor, and grab the hem of my shirt in both hands, lifting it over my head. My nipples are tight, achy peaks under my bra. If I had any question whether or not Lukas could see them, the quiet groan of "Fuck me," would be a dead giveaway. My heart is beating so hard I feel like it could break right out of my chest. I want him. And I love that he wants me just as badly.

Lukas pushes off the door frame and brushes his wet hair back with his fingertips as he stalks over to me. He doesn't hesitate for even

67

a second. He leans down and kisses me, his mouth claiming mine. Every cell in my body screams *"yes, yes, YES,"* as he wraps an arm around my back, holding me tight against his chest. His skin feels as chilled as mine, his face cold against mine, but his mouth is warm. He walks me backward, kissing me so hard it feels like he's stealing the air from my lungs.

His body wraps around mine as we move, possessive and powerful. I love the way he steers me around, moving me, and holding me close at the same time. My back hits the glass shower panel, and it's *freezing*. A violent shiver racks my body. Lukas breaks the kiss, pulling back to look at me, concern carving little lines around his mouth and eyes.

"Jesus, your lips are blue," he mutters as he reaches into the shower and cranks the water on, holding a hand under the water to test the temperature. I kick my shoes off and peel my soggy jeans down my hips. *Note to self: wet denim is not a sexy thing to strip out of.*

Lukas watches me, a needy growl ripping its way out of his throat. He reaches back and yanks his shirt off. I hear a couple stitches pop and I'm half surprised he didn't just rip it off like the Hulk. He shoves his jeans and boxers down with zero shame.

Not that he has anything to be ashamed of. Jesus, God in heaven.

I was supposed to be doing something, but I am completely distracted by the erection he just unleashed in this tiny room. He's thick and hard, veins winding up the length to a broad head.

"So… do you need a special license to operate that thing?" I ask breathlessly.

Lukas runs his fingers through his hair. He's trying to contain the smug smile playing at the edge of his lips but losing the battle.

"Get in the shower, smart ass."

"Okay, bossy," I say as I reach back to unhook my bra slowly, still eyeing his package. I lick my lips, wondering how it would feel against my tongue. Would he make that growly sound when I took him in my mouth? I've never done it before… but now I really want to. At least, I want to with him.

"You're fucking killing me with that look," he says. Without warning, he ducks down and presses into my middle, throwing me over his shoulder. I yelp in surprise as he carries me into the shower. I'm still wearing my bra and panties when he steps under the hot water. It's shocking as it runs down my back, sending little pinpricks over my skin. Lukas sets me on my feet, rubbing my arms like he's trying to erase the goosebumps that dot my skin.

I grab his bicep and pull him closer, sharing the hot water. It runs between our bodies; the spray beading up on his face as he looks down at me. Lukas slides a hand to the back of my neck as he takes me in. There's a predatory heat in his eyes that makes it hard for me to breathe.

"You are so goddamn beautiful." His voice rumbles through me, eliciting an entirely different kind of shiver before his lips crash into mine. There's nothing gentle in the way he kisses me. His tongue pushes past my parted lips, teasing mine. I kiss him back, surrendering to his hold over me. It feels too good to fight, anyway.

Lukas bites my lower lip, pulling on it and sending a tingle of awareness through my body. I never thought I'd like that, but my clit throbs in response, and I moan against his lips. His erection flexes against my belly, begging to be touched. Tentatively, I reach down and run my fingers up the length of it. He's hot and heavy and I love the feel of his veins. I can feel the blood throbbing just under the surface and it's so flipping sexy. Closing my fist around him, I slide my hand up and down, slicked by the water.

He groans my name and I can just imagine him making that sound as he sinks into me. Lukas reaches around me and unhooks my bra with a flick of his fingers before sliding it down my arms. It hits the floor of the shower with a wet thud and a nervous giggle bubbles up in my throat. I feel a flash of vulnerability, but it's washed away when Lukas cups my breast, the pad of his thumb rasping over my nipple, rolling and circling. His breathing is ragged as his mouth moves down my neck, warm breath mixing with the steam of the shower. The passionate kisses are peppered with sharp little bites and licks and it all swirls together in mind-numbing pleasure.

His warm lips close around my nipple, sucking and flicking at it with his tongue.

"Lukas!" I gasp. Holy mother that feels good. His cock throbs in my hand and his teeth scrape the tip of my nipple. "Oh my God," I whimper. My heart is pounding in my chest, fueled by pleasure and lust.

Lukas presses my back to the wall and sinks to his knees in front of me, kissing and biting my hip. He grips my panties at one side, shredding them. "Holy hell," I whisper as his fists grip the other side, the muscles in his forearm flexing as he destroys the fabric and throws my ruined panties across the shower.

He gazes up at me, his eyes dark and clouded with lust as he runs his fingertips from the back of my ankle and up my calf.

"You ever let a man eat this pretty pussy, Parker?" he asks, his voice gruff.

I lick my lips and swallow hard. I'm shaking and I can't breathe or speak, but I give my head a jerky shake. I might as well just admit that I'm probably one of the most inexperienced women he'll ever meet. My entire sexual history could probably be replayed, in real-time, in under nine minutes.

"Are you going to let me?" Lukas gives me a devilish grin as he runs a finger over the curls shielding my pussy. He barely touches me, but it sends sparks to every nerve ending in my body and I nod, a little frantically. I always assumed that was something men only did in books, but I'm sure as hell not going to complain. I think I'd let him do anything he wants right now.

Lukas grasps the back of my knee in his hand and lifts it over his shoulder, watching my face the whole time. I feel like a deer in the headlights, frozen and waiting to see what's coming. Me. Oh God, I hope it's me.

He wraps his arm around my thigh, holding me in place and exposed as his gaze sweeps down my body. He leans in, nuzzles his nose into my curls, and I realize I'm trembling in anticipation. I feel a finger stroke over me before parting my folds. I'm so wet that it's embarrassing. I'm praying he'll just assume it's from the shower. I mean, I know the difference, but I don't know if he can tell.

Lukas slicks his fingers through the moisture and circles my clit. My breathing stutters as the warmth flows through me. It feels *so good.* So much better than when I touch myself. He slips a finger inside me as his tongue drags over my clit and I moan, grabbing his hair. I need something to anchor me or I might just float away on that feeling. He chuckles, and the sound vibrates through my aching clit. His tongue circles and flicks as his thick finger thrusts in and out of me, stirring desire deep in my core.

I lean against the tiled wall, letting it support me as I roll my hips against his mouth. Lukas seems to like that because he growls against my clit, his grip tightening on my thigh. A second finger presses inside me, filling and stretching me with blinding pleasure.

14

LUKAS

Mine.

Parker tastes like goddamn heaven. I don't care what it takes to convince her, but I'm going to eat this pussy every day for the rest of my fucking life. A pink flush spreads over her body as she rocks against my mouth, urgent little gasps escaping each time I push my fingers into her. My hand is coated in her slick honey, the faint smell of musk and peaches filling the surrounding air.

It's everything I can do to keep from blowing my load on the shower floor, but the only place I want to come is buried deep inside this woman, her legs wrapped around me, and my name on her pretty lips.

I curl my fingers into her g-spot, pressing and stroking as her sweet pussy clasps me tight. She's drenched for me and I fucking love it. Little moans slip out on panted breaths.

"Lukas—" she gasps, gripping my hair so hard that tiny pricks of pain spread across my scalp. I don't care. She can rip every hair out of my head as long as I get to feel her come on my tongue. I suck her clit between my lips, holding it as her legs shake and her pussy ripples around my fingers.

"Oh, God. Lukas... I—" Parker cries out and I growl against her clit and suck harder. Her back arches and she nearly comes off the wall. She lets out a keening wail and fresh moisture slicks my fingers as she comes, hips jerking, body trembling.

There's a dreamy look on her face when I slip my fingers from her that makes my heart beat so hard it hurts. A curl of possessive satisfaction roars through me. Mine. That look is mine. Her sighs and moans are *mine*. This pussy is mine and no one but me will ever taste it. I turn my head to kiss the smooth skin of her inner thigh, sucking the skin between my teeth and marking her.

Am I a bastard? Maybe. But no one will see her and think she's fair game, and that thought fills me with pleasure.

She moans as I move my mouth to a new spot and runs her hands through my hair, encouraging me to do it again. I leave a trail of love bites up her leg before easing her foot back to the floor. Parker's eyes are hooded with lust, her lips slack as she watches me stand. I trail my fingertips over the curves of her hips and up her sides. Her skin is flushed and warm under my hands, the goosebumps and shivering long gone.

"You're beautiful like this," I tell her. It sounds trite, but I mean it. Nothing compares to the sight of her. The water beading up and trailing down her soft curves in fascinating paths, her breasts rising towards me with each breath she takes. Parker watches me from under her eyelashes, her little cupid's bow lips parted as her eyes dart away like she doesn't quite believe me. Fuck that.

Grasping her chin, I lift her face, forcing her to look up at me as I press my body against hers. My cock is pinned between us and I'm so hard that it's throbbing against her soft stomach. Her hands rest on my chest, her fingers stroking my chest hair cautiously. I love her soft touches as much as the hard, desperate way she clung to me while I ate her out. I want to sink into her tight pussy so bad it hurts. She has to know how badly I want her, right? How fucking desperate I am to be inside her. To be part of her.

Her blue eyes meet mine and I can see uncertainty; the doubt clouding her face makes me ache in a completely different way. She looks so small, so vulnerable. I lower my face over hers, so close I can feel her breath warming my skin.

"Why do I feel like you don't believe me?" I ask.

"I…" she stutters and swallows before speaking again. "I'm just not used to hearing that, I guess."

"Get used to it," I say, my lips brushing over hers. "You're so goddamn beautiful that it hurts to look at you sometimes. I get a semi when you walk into the room." I flex my dick against her stomach just to emphasize the point, and it makes her laugh.

Kissing her softly, I draw her lower lip between my teeth. Parker moans softly against me and deepens the kiss. I claim her mouth, loving the way she opens for me, inviting me. Her hand slides down my chest, fingertips scraping over my stomach as she moves lower. Her touch is tentative as she strokes the edge of my erection. I want to feel her little fist wrap around me, pump me until I come all over her. Her gentle fingers swirl around the head and I groan into the kiss. Her soft touches feel incredible, better than they have any right to.

Parker pulls her chin down and I'm ready to hear her say she wants to slow down, that she wants to stop, that this is too much. But if there's one thing I'm learning about Parker, it's that she likes to keep me on my toes.

"I want to do that for you too," she says, as her fingers wrap around the head of my cock.

"Do what?" I ask, suppressing a smile. I know what she means, but I want to hear her say it. Parker licks her lips and her mouth moves, but no words come out. I lower my head, putting my lips next to her ear. "You want to put that pretty mouth on my cock, Parker?" I whisper.

Her body trembles as she nods.

"I want to hear you say it. Tell me all the dirty things you want, baby girl."

A tiny moan escapes her throat. "I want to put you in my mouth," she whispers as she drops to her knees. I angle my shoulders so the water doesn't spray in her face as I stroke my dick, trying to ease the ache.

"Tell me you want to suck my cock," I demand. I need to hear those filthy words come out of her innocent lips.

Parker looks up at me, baby blues peeking out from under her long lashes. "I want to suck your cock."

"Good girl," I growl. Parker places her palms on my thighs and eyes my cock, equal parts hungry and unsure. "You've never done this either, have you?" I ask her. That familiar, possessive pleasure floods my bloodstream when she shakes her head. *Mine. Only mine.*

"Open your mouth," I say. Her eyes are wide with excitement as she licks her lips, parting them. I press the head of my cock against her mouth. "Suck it."

Parker's breathing hard and her pretty eyes are locked on mine as she wraps her lips around my cock, sucking it gently. Her tongue strokes the underside of the head and I suck in a hard breath. Fuck, that feels good. It's all I can do to hold still and let her take her time. She bobs her head just a little and looks at me inquisitively as if testing my reaction.

"That's so good, baby," I tell her, my voice raspy. I run a hand along her jaw and behind her neck, tunneling my hand into her wet hair, holding it away from her face. She moans around my cock and the vibration is pure pleasure. Her fingertips grip my thighs, flexing as she moves her mouth up and down my shaft, taking me deeper on each stroke. She pushes so far that I feel my dick hit the back of her throat and my knees nearly give out. Parker moans as she pulls back, swirling her tongue around the head and sucking me back in.

"Oh, fuck," I mutter. "You're so good with that mouth, baby." She makes a pleased humming noise that feels incredible. Tension pulls in my abdomen. I'm strung too tight and I'm afraid I'll snap. As amazing as her mouth feels, I need to be inside her, really inside her, when I come.

I grab a handful of Parker's hair, gently pulling her back before she makes me lose control completely. She lets my dick go with a little pop and a worried look on her face.

"Did I do it wrong?" she asks.

I grab her elbow and pull her back to her feet. "Hell no."

15

PARKER

Lukas pulls me off his cock and to my feet so quickly that I'm afraid I hurt him. Did he hate it that much? Maybe it was a bad idea to try my first blow job in the shower.

"Did I do it wrong?" I ask. Maybe I could try it again?

"Hell no," he says before settling his mouth on mine, kissing me with so much passion and need that it steals my breath. Simmering desire spreads through my body, lighting my nerves up with an uncontrollable craving. I feel achy and empty and the wicked need to be filled just grows and grows.

Lukas cups my jaw in one hand as he pulls back. The pad of his thumb caresses my lips and they feel hot and swollen under his touch.

"I want to take you to bed, Parker," he says. "I want to fuck you so good you can't remember your own name." His eyes are gentle and the reverent look he's giving me is at complete odds with the dirty talk, but I love it. My whole body tingles at the thought of him pressing inside, filling me.

"Yes, please," I whisper, throwing my arms around his neck. Lukas grabs my ass and picks me up. I wrap my legs around his hips and let him claim my mouth, loving the way his body flexes and moves with mine. He slams a hand down on the faucet, shutting off the water and stepping out of the shower door. His fingers dig into my ass cheeks as he carries me, dripping wet, to the bedroom and sets me on the edge of the bed.

He steps away, grabbing a condom from the bureau behind him, and eyes me with dark hunger as he opens it and slowly rolls it down his erection. I watch in fascination. I don't know if a penis is supposed to be beautiful, but his really is. That bulging ridge along the head is especially toe-curling, and I'm not entirely sure why. It just seems to fit him. He's thick all over and I kind of love that his cock matches.

Lukas spreads my legs, stepping between them, his hips pressing my thighs wide so he can fit.

"What about this, Parker? You been with a man like this?"

I bite my lip. Like this? Hell no. But I know what he means. He's asking if I'm a virgin and I'm not.

"Once," I answer quietly. Lukas shrugs and gives me a cocky smile.

"If I can't be first, I can be the best."

I grin back at him because that might be the most 'Lukas' answer on the face of the planet and I freaking love it.

He presses a hand to the center of my chest, pushing me back on the bed before trailing it down between the V of my breasts, over my stomach, and down my leg. I love that he's not overly gentle with me. He's not so rough that I'm worried he'd hurt me, but every movement is firm and it's obvious he thinks he's in charge.

I lean up on my elbows so I can watch his hands move over my body. They're huge and his skin is a deep golden tan. There's something so erotic about the manliness of his hands. He takes one of my knees and drapes it over his shoulder. I'm completely exposed to his gaze and his eyes are glued to my sex. Lukas licks his lips and all I can think about is the way his mouth felt on me. His thumb brushes over my sensitive clit and it feels so good I nearly come off the bed. I wrap my free leg around the back of his hips, pulling him as close as he'll let me.

He grips his sheathed cock in one hand, pressing it against my entrance. The anticipation is killing me. I feel like a live wire, getting jumpier and more frantic with every second he makes me wait. His thumb rubs little circles on my clit as his hips push forward and I can't help but gasp when he enters me. He's so big that the sensation is overwhelming. I have to fight to keep my eyes open as he works his way into me, stretching me inch by inch. Tendrils of pleasure swirl through my core as I watch him stroke in and out, moving deeper with every thrust until he's sinking every blessed inch of his cock inside me.

"Look at me, Parker," Lukas demands. His voice is low, and he makes a growly sound in his throat when my eyes meet his.

"Oh God," I breathe out. That's so insanely sexy.

Lukas is shaking when he leans down and presses his forehead to mine. His green eyes bore into me and I'm captivated by the desperate hunger in them. Every touch feels like he's claiming me, possessing me, and marking me as his.

"So good," he murmurs against my lips. "You feel so fucking good."

I nod frantically.

"Tell me," he growls.

"You're so big," I moan as he plunges into me. I love the demanding, animalistic edge in his voice. My core clenches around him. "I'm so full. So wet," I whimper.

"Fuck," he mutters.

His hand slips from my shoulder to the column of my throat, holding me in place as he thrusts into me. He doesn't squeeze, just holds me in his huge hand. It's so possessive, so powerful and, God help me, I love it. I shiver, the pleasure spreading through me, my core tightening in response. I was wet before, but I am quickly reaching embarrassing levels of moisture.

"Sorry," he mutters, moving his hand back to my shoulder as he kisses me.

"I liked it," I tell him quietly, our lips grazing, breaths shared.

Lukas pulls back a couple of inches to look me in the eyes. Those dazzling green eyes searching mine. "Yeah?"

I can't believe I said that but… I *really* liked it. I suck my bottom lip between my teeth and nod.

Lukas wraps a hand behind my neck, gripping the sides in his thick fingers, and the tension in my lower stomach ratchets even higher. His thumb slides through the moisture seeping out of my pussy.

"Damn baby, you *really* like that, don't you? Look at this wet pussy." He lifts his thumb to his mouth, sucking the moisture off. My clit throbs with my racing heart, aching for his touch. His fingers tighten slightly as he swipes a finger over my clit, bringing the glistening finger to my mouth and pressing it against my tongue.

"Lick," he commands, watching my face, his eyes hooded with lust. I wrap my tongue around the digit and suck, panting in exhilaration. It's so filthy, so dirty, so beyond what I expected, and it's fucking sexy as hell.

Lukas wiggles the fingers on his other hand, reminding me that he's holding me by the throat as he thrusts into me, deliberate and powerful. I moan around his finger as my pussy clenches. The tingling beginnings of an orgasm prick my skin and make the edges of my vision shimmer.

"You going to come for me, Parker? Be a dirty girl for me. Come on my cock."

He pulls his finger from my mouth, dragging it over my lower lip. His fingers slip down to my pussy, slicking them around our joined bodies before swirling them around my sensitive bundle of nerves. The pleasure builds until I'm shaking and my pulse thunders in my ears. Lukas leans back, lifting my butt off the bed and stroking hard, my back arches and he holds me in his firm grasp as I fall apart. All I can feel is blinding pleasure, the jerking thrusts of his release, and his fingers on my neck, anchoring me to him as everything else melts away.

I float back into my body slowly. My body feels wrung out in the best way, but emotionally I feel raw. Lukas kisses me on the forehead, holding me close a moment before slipping out of me with a groan. He stands up and I instantly feel cold and empty.

"Give me a sec," he says before heading into the bathroom, presumably to get rid of the condom. I hear water running in a sink as I look around. I'm chilly without his body heat, so I grab the comforter and wrap it around my shoulders. Should I go? I don't know what the etiquette is here. I mean, I guess I can't go anywhere. I don't have a car and my clothes are in a soaking wet heap in Lukas' bathroom.

I'm worrying my lip between my teeth, mulling over my lack of options when Lukas strides back into the bedroom, buck naked. It's the first time I've had a chance to really look at him without all the distracting, frantic sexual need. Don't get me wrong, it's simmering under the surface, but two earth-shattering orgasms seem to have dulled it, at least temporarily.

Tattoos cover both arms. A pirate ship being tossed about by giant waves and a kraken wrap one arm and shoulder. An atlas covers his other arm, layered with beautifully rendered objects. I want to hold him still and examine every inch, but from here I can see a pocket watch, skulls, a compass, and roses all in black ink. The feathered wing I saw under his shirt collar earlier connects to a raven on his back and wraps around to his chest, each feather drawn in careful detail. He is just insanely gorgeous, head to toe, and next to him I feel so... average.

"You ok, Freckles?" he asks, running a hand through his hair, pulling it out of his face. His emerald eyes search mine.

I nod and smile at him, faking confidence I don't feel. "Yeah, just realizing I don't have clothes to change into."

He smirks at my bare legs, still hanging over the edge of the bed. I'm pressing my thighs together, mostly because of out-of-place modesty. He's seen (and licked) just about every inch of me in the last hour. It's probably dumb to cover up now.

"I'm perfectly fine with the state you're in," he says, wiggling a knee between mine and stepping into my personal space. He cups my face in both hands and turns my face up to his, kissing me deeply until my worries evaporate and I melt into him. He holds my face and searches my eyes with his. "Would you be more comfortable in one of my shirts while I dry your clothes?"

I smile up at Lukas and nod. He kisses me on the forehead before grabbing a black t-shirt out of the dresser behind him. He unfolds it and gives it a little shake before pulling it over my head. He grins at me while I toss the blanket back, pulling my arms through the holes.

"Looks better on you than it does on me anyway," he says with a wink before turning back to the bathroom. "I'll toss your clothes in the dryer so you have something to wear in the morning. That ok with you?" he asks.

"Y-yah..." I stutter, staring at his ass as he walks away. I didn't realize I was an ass girl until this exact second, but holy shiitake mushrooms. Two perfect globes of man-butt go swinging away, and I half expect a chorus of angels to start singing. I have to lean sideways to keep a clear line of sight, and when he bends over to collect our discarded clothing, I lean a little too far and fall right off the damn bed, pulling the comforter with me.

Lukas whips around with a startled expression on his face. "You ok, Freckles?"

I laugh awkwardly, trying to stand and untangle myself from the blanket, stalling while I come up with an excuse. Was I staring at his glorious ham hocks? You betcha. But I'm sure as hell not telling him that.

"I think my foot just got tangled in the blanket. I'm fine," I say breathlessly as he strides back over, holding out a hand to help me up. Jesus Christ. The front view isn't helping me compose myself either.

16

LUKAS

It's nearly impossible not to smirk at Parker, flustered and adorable as she tries to hide the fact that she fell out of bed because she was staring at my ass. As if I couldn't see her in the mirror, leaning out farther and farther as I walked into the bathroom. The covetous look on her face was enough to stroke my ego to completion. That pretty mouth hanging open, eyes wide as her tongue played with her upper teeth. It would be enough to make any man feel like a god. So maybe I flexed and gave her a little show as I bent over. I was just trying to work my best angle; I didn't expect her to topple right off the bed.

"I'm fine," she mutters, avoiding eye contact and untangling herself from the blanket.

"I'll say," I tease back, taking her hand and helping her to her feet before reaching around to grab a handful of her sexy-as-fuck ass under my t-shirt. She giggles but doesn't pull away. Parker wraps her arms around my neck and grins at me, pink spreading across her cheeks. I love the way she blushes, giving away those inner dirty thoughts I know she's trying to hide.

"Look, I know it's hard, but try not to look at my ass when I walk away. I'd feel terrible if you got hurt just because you couldn't control yourself."

Parker sputters and the color staining her cheeks deepens. "I wasn't... I mean, I didn't—"

I grab her hips and pop her back on the bed before giving her a quick kiss and putting her out of her misery. "I like it, Freckles. Stay here, I'll be right back."

I pull on a pair of boxers before scooping up our wet clothes from the bathroom floor, making eye contact in the mirror with a guilty-looking Parker as I bend over. She laughs and covers her face.

"Yeah, ok. I'm busted." Her voice is muffled through her fingers.

I give her a quick kiss and run downstairs and throw the clothes in the dryer but pause when I see her bra on top of the pile. I've never done a woman's laundry before, but I remember my sisters hung their bras up all over the house as teenagers. It was horrifying to thirteen-year-old me, but they all did it, so I'm guessing most chicks don't put their bras in the dryer. I snatch Parker's bra back out and hang it on the hook by the back door where I put my keys.

Peering in the fridge, I pull out two beers. I don't have shit for decent snacks in the house and I doubt post-coital Doritos are very romantic. Beer will have to do. I take the stairs back up two at a time, pausing in the doorway. Parker is curled up under the blanket on one side of the bed, looking tired. I climb in bed next to her, twist the cap off the beer, and hand it to her. She sips it and looks at me shyly. I raise an eyebrow at her and take a long swig from mine. I love that even after I ate her pussy in the shower and fucked her over the edge of the bed, she's still getting flustered.

"Alright, fine," she mutters. "I don't know what I'm doing here. What's the etiquette on this?"

I choke on my beer. "The etiquette?" I ask.

Her nose scrunches up and she looks straight ahead of her. "Yes, the etiquette! I mean, I can't exactly get out of your hair without clothes or a car. I don't know what side of the bed I should be on. Do you want me to go sleep in the guest bed or something?"

The laugh erupts out of my chest, uncontrollable and unrestrained. "Are you serious right now? You keep your cute ass right here in my bed. You can have either side. Hell, you can sleep right in the middle if you want."

She laughs, visibly relaxing.

"Come here. At the risk of sounding like a pussy, I would really like to hold you," I tell her, pulling her closer so I can put my arm around her. Parker sets her beer on the side table and rests her head on my shoulder, snuggling in and resting her arm across my stomach.

She mutters, "pussy" under her breath and giggles.

"Smart ass."

I stroke my fingers up and down the back of her arm and kiss the top of her head. This is it for me. I don't know how I know it, but I do. She feels perfect. I can't remember a time I wanted to hold someone like this but here I am. I've been getting these little moments all day where I can feel how right this is with her. Plus, sex has *never* felt like that before. It's never been about anything but plea-sure before; but this... holy shit. I feel like a teenage girl just thinking about it like this, but it was like we were a part of each other.

"Can I ask you something personal?" I ask her.

She laughs and smacks me on the chest. "Well, considering how *personal* we've gotten in the last few hours, yeah. I'd say you can."

"You really are a smart ass under that candy shell, aren't you?"

Parker doesn't answer, but she smirks and raises an eyebrow at me, shrugging.

"You've really only had sex once before this?" I ask her.

Parker tenses, sitting up to grab her beer. "That is definitely personal. I don't think you really want to know the specifics on this." She takes a long pull from the beer, her eyes looking everywhere but at me.

"Well, now I definitely need to know."

She shakes her head slowly as she looks up at the ceiling. "I mean, you already guessed it at the bar. Lights off, missionary position. Although it was less making love and more like two minutes of inept fumbling. I snuck out to go to a party and hooked up with a townie. It was a total mistake, but it's not like you can take that back, right?"

I wince at the look on her face and feel like a real asshole for even bringing this up. "I'm sorry, I shouldn't have asked. If it makes you feel any better, everyone's first time sucks. It's a universal truth."

Parker peeks at me out of the corner of her eye, her lips pursed in disbelief, "I highly doubt your first time sucked."

"It was horrible," I tell her with a laugh.

"I don't believe you," she says primly.

I run my hands through my hair and chug the last of my beer. It's my turn to look at the ceiling and try to put the whole experience into words.

"Sadie Jones was Lilah's best friend in high school. She was a year older than me and I thought she was the hottest thing this side of the Sierra Nevada's, but she never noticed me. Not for years. Not until I hit a growth spurt and bulked out. It was like, overnight, she was all over me every time she came around. I was too young and stupid to know any better, so we started going out. It was just a bonus that it pissed off my sister. Young and stupid, keep that in mind, please."

Parker laughs and relaxes into my side again. "Got it, young and stupid. The mantra of the teenage boy."

"Exactly. So, a couple months in, Sadie decides we should have sex. I was a teenage boy, so I thought she deserved a Nobel prize for that idea."

Parker covers her face with her hands. "What happened?" she asks, voice muffled.

Scrubbing a hand over my face, I tell her the truth. "I couldn't really... get it up."

"Nuh-uh!"

"Yeah. She was slobbering everywhere and making these annoying fake moaning sounds. It was like she watched the worst porn she could find and then copied it. Which, in hindsight, I'm almost certain she did."

Parker laughs behind her hands and makes a sympathetic groan. Her hair is starting to dry in wild pale coppery waves and they tickle my bicep.

"Okay, that's— that's pretty awful."

"That's not even the worst part," I tell her. "Sadie was so offended by what she perceived as my lack of interest, that she told everyone that I took her virginity and then dumped her."

Parker gasps in outrage. "What a bitch!"

85

I whip my head down to look at Parker. "I don't think I've ever actually heard you swear like that."

"I swear. I'm just judicious about it," she grins back at me before yawning.

"Well, it's adorable," I say before reaching to turn off the light.

Parker settles in next to me, her head on my shoulder, a warm hand resting on my chest. Reaching down, I slide my hand over one gorgeous ass cheek and down to her knee so I can hitch her leg over my thighs. Light from streetlamps trickles through the blinds, and I can see the little freckles that dot Parker's thigh. I trace their path with my fingertips.

Perfect. This feels absolutely perfect. A possessive thought overtakes me. My family is going to jump all over us as soon as they find out. I'm not ready for that. I want to keep her all to myself, at least for a little while.

The worst part is, I know it won't be long before my family finds out. I love my sisters and Gran, but they are nosy as hell and have opinions spilling out of their ears, especially Lilah. I'd be surprised if Gran doesn't know I took Parker to Anita's by now. At least Gran probably won't say anything until family dinner, which gives me almost a week to figure this out.

But my sisters... they'll talk to Parker before then. I get the impression they see each other nearly every day. Would she say anything to them? If I was any other guy, she probably would. Shit. That could ruin everything. Lilah might try to talk her out of seeing me again. Probably tell her all the worst things I've done and all the awful things she suspects me of.

Parker isn't a pushover and I doubt she would let anyone talk her out of doing what she wants to do, but... I can't bear the thought of someone poisoning this. This thing between us is real. I just need more time to make Parker see how special it is and show her I'm more than just a good time. If I can just keep everyone else out of it until Parker feels the way I feel... that would be best, right?

17

PARKER

I think this is what heaven must feel like. I'm warm, sated, and draped all over the sexiest man on the face of the planet. Lukas has a proprietary hand on my thigh, his fingers tracing little patterns over my skin. Moonlight is streaming through the cracks in the blinds, shafts of light illuminating bits and pieces of the feathers tattooed on his chest.

Stroking the delicate lines that flow out from each wing, I close my eyes, enjoying the feel of his chest rising under my hand. I almost can't believe this is where I am right now. Twenty-four hours ago I was lying awake, cursing Lukas for his douche-baggery at the bar.

I'm just drifting off when his voice pulls me back. "We can keep this just between us, right?"

My eyes fly open, but the rest of me freezes solid. A lead weight crashing through the peace. I am such an idiot. "Yeah, I... Of course."

It's not like I was going to go run through the streets yelling, "I slept with Lukas Donovan!" But clearly, I didn't think this through. I got so swept up in him I didn't think about the consequences of sleeping with my best friend's brother.

I can't believe I did this to myself. I've been twisting this whole day into a grand romanticized adventure. I mean, it's what I always wanted, right? To be swept away on the back of a motorcycle by a tall, dark, and handsome bad boy? The beach was just the cherry on top of the Parker-seduction sundae that Lukas brought to the table. I got swept away in a fantasy of my own making.

Obviously, we have chemistry, but Lukas made it pretty clear he wasn't going to pursue it. He was perfectly happy to go shower in the other room until I *asked* him to stay. I threw myself at him and the worst part is, I *knew* better. It's not like he hid anything from me.

So, what exactly did I think was going to happen? That he'd fall for me? That we'd get a golden retriever and a picket fence? Pop out some pretty little babies and live happily ever after? All because he was nice to me for one evening instead of the flaming asshole I've come to expect. I thought I'd misjudged him, but really, I am just an idiot. A naïve, romantic idiot.

This is almost so tragic it's funny. Did I think I could change him? Am I that much of a cliche? Well, hell. I guess I am. I honestly thought we had a real connection. That the sex we shared was more than just physical, but that's ridiculous. I'm just so inexperienced that one good lay sent me over the deep end.

I'm not sure how long I lay in bed, frozen in place, trying to sort through the day without the rose-colored glasses. To see it from his point of view. He was just trying to be nice, and I made it into so much more in my head.

Lukas is sleeping peacefully, his chest rising and falling in a relaxed rhythm under my arm. He's still holding my thigh, his calloused fingers curled around the back of my leg. Oh, my freaking god. Even in sleep, he's turning me on. It's really not fair.

Carefully, I tip my chin up so I can see his face. I totally know why I fell for the fantasy when I look at him like this. His dark hair is tousled over one side of his face, there's something vaguely exotic about the turn of his eyes, and oh lord, that jaw with those full lips. He's officially my brand of catnip; I just want to rub myself all over him and make bad choices.

I need to get out of here. If I wake up next to him, I know I'll do anything he wants. If he's conscious, I won't be able to resist him and then I'll hate myself for being weak. As amazing as this was, I don't want to be someone's dirty little secret. I know I deserve better than that. I just have to find it in myself to be stronger than the pull I feel towards him. Even if the thought of leaving makes me feel sick to my stomach.

From somewhere in the dark of the house, I hear the dryer buzz. Well, there's my sign, right? My clothes are ready, so I better put on my grown-up panties (figuratively, since he tore my panties to shreds) and get out of here.

Gently, I lift Lukas' hand from my leg, ignoring the cold stabbing sensation in my chest. He shifts as I extricate myself from his arms and reaches for me again.

"Where goin'?" he asks sleepily, eyes still closed.

"Bathroom. Go back to sleep," I soothe as I slip from the bed while guilt rips my chest open.

"Miss you..." he mumbles, throwing an arm over a pillow.

I'm trying to contain the tears that are threatening to spill from the corners of my eyes. *Me too*, I think. At least, I'll miss the idea of him, but I need to grow the hell up and face reality. New Parker is a hell of a lot of fun, but she's shit at decision making.

I pad to the bathroom, retrieving my damp purse. My phone is dry, at least. I wait to get downstairs to open it and pull up the rideshare app. It's only a little past midnight, so I guess there are still plenty of drivers out. The app says Kevin will be here in seven minutes. *Clothes*! I can't exactly walk outside in a t-shirt, sans panties.

It takes way too long to locate the washer and dryer. My jeans are warm and dry so I pull those on at breakneck speed, shoving my tank top in my purse, but my stupid bra is nowhere to be found. I dig around in the dryer, but all I can find are Lukas' clothes. Frantically, I search the area, but it's not in the washer or on the floor either. Damn. The app shows Kevin is just around the corner. I can't risk him honking or waking Lukas up. I guess the bra is a goner. That really sucks. I only have two more and I don't like them as much.

Cursing my poor sleuthing skills, I quietly slip out the front door, making sure it's locked behind me. I climb into the black Prius, painfully aware of how walk-of-shame-y I look. Messy hair and braless in a men's shirt? Yeah. I'm not fooling anyone here. The frat boy driver has the decency not to say anything about it. Just offers me a complimentary bottle of water and confirms my address. I pass on the water, cross my arms over my chest, and stare out the window in silence until we pull up in front of my house.

"Have a nice night. If you get a chance, could you give me a five-star review?" Kevin asks as I step out of the car.

"Sure. Thanks," I mumble before closing the door. My foot barely hits the curb before the tears start falling. Cujo is waiting for me, front paws perched on top of the neighbor's gate. Apparently, he's not going to sneak up on me tonight, which is just as well. I don't think I could take the jump-scare right now. He's wiggling, excited to see me, but his puppy smile is missing and he's whimpering.

"Hey buddy," I say, scratching him behind the ears. His expressive eyebrows look almost worried as he licks the tears from my face. "At least I know you love me," I say sadly. He whimpers again, dancing his paws on top of the chain link, trying to get closer to me. I look up and down the street. All the houses are dark... this is probably a terrible idea, but I kind of need the affection right now. I wince and lift the latch on Cujo's gate, praying it won't squeak. The Rottweiler sits as I open it, watching me. The second I sit on the hard-packed dirt, he's all over me, wiggling and whining and licking my face.

"Good boy," I laugh quietly through my tears. He crawls all of his solid doggy muscle into my lap and sits on me, letting me cry into his neck. This has to be the purest, sweetest affection I've ever received from a living creature, and the thought just makes me sob harder. I'm so tired of being alone. Maybe that's why I built up this evening with Lukas in my head. It's definitely the reason it hurt so much when I realized how wrong I was.

"I should have brought you a taco," I tell him once I've cried myself out. He just stares into my eyes and licks my nose. "Next time, I promise. I'll get you a whole pile of shredded pork." A car drives by at the end of the street and makes me jump. The last thing I need is to get caught in a possible dognapping.

"Come on, buddy. Let's get you home." I pat Cujo's side and he obediently gets off my lap with one last lick. I'm going to need another shower but it was worth it. Getting to my feet and brushing the dirt off my pants, I point at Cujo's yard. He looks hangdog but goes through the gate. I make sure the latch is secure before heading towards my tiny...Fuck it. It's a shed tonight. Cujo walks along the fence line with me, whining all the way.

I TRY TO SLEEP. I really do. I toss and turn on my hard, creaky mattress for hours. I close my eyes and try to empty my mind. I follow a guided meditation I find on YouTube. I google breathing exercises for relaxation.

No matter what I try, all I can think about is Lukas. Filthy, possessive, sexy Lukas. His body moving over mine. His hand on my neck...

Miss you.

The sweet, peaceful expression on his face as he slept. I wonder how he'll react when he wakes up and I'm gone...

NOPE!

He'll be fine. He'll probably be relieved.

I finally give up on sleep and get in the shower. I can still smell Lukas on me, and I'm sure that's not helping anything. I shampoo my hair twice and almost forget to use conditioner. The water goes cold halfway through rinsing it out, but I really don't care. I dry off and grab a dress at random, throwing it on over my head in an exhausted fog.

I have to get another ride downtown, so I wait outside and pet Cujo over the fence while I wait in the pre-dawn light for the car. An older woman with a voice that speaks of decades of chain smoking picks me up. She's grumpier than Kevin and pretty much ignores me for the duration of the drive. My mood matches hers so that suits me just fine. I just hope I can get Lilah to drop me off this evening.

Groaning inwardly, I realize I'm going to have to interact with the Donovan sisters and somehow keep all of this to myself. I'm terrible at keeping secrets and putting on a happy face when I don't feel it. And it won't help that I look like hell. My face is puffy from crying and a complete lack of sleep. Maybe I can claim an allergy attack? They might buy that... as long as I don't weep openly.

I exit the car with a muttered, "Thanks." It's the least polite I can stand to be, even in a crappy mood. I unlock the front door of my shop but don't step inside. It's dark and empty and I feel miserable just looking at it. Behind me the lights are shining out of Olive Branch Bakery and I can see Olive and Lilah in the dining room, drinking coffee and laughing. My stomach churns. I've never felt so far on the outside.

Even during the long miserable years I spent growing up in Middle River, I had my books and the single-minded, if naïve, focus of a girl looking forward to a better life. I had plans. I had an escape and hope. I didn't know what it was like to have friends like Olive, Lilah, and Julia, and I definitely didn't know what I was missing when it came to sex.

Now I have too much to lose, so much to miss. And my books won't be any consolation right now. I can't bear the thought of reading someone else's happily ever after when I feel like this. How can all those stories turn out like that? Piles and piles of happy couples with their beautiful stories and perfect endings. It feels like a lie.

I watch my friends for too long. I should have gone inside when I had the chance because Lilah looks up and waves me over the second she spots me. I'm not ready to face them, but if I ignore her, they'll know something is wrong and come check on me. If I go over there, I can at least duck out quickly and say I need to do inventory or something.

Bracing myself, I lock the door again and cross the street. Olive greets me at the door with a cup of coffee and a hug.

"You look like shit. What are you doing here so early?"

I laugh and take the coffee. If there's one thing I love about the Donovan girls, it's the way they don't mince words.

"Allergies are killing me and I've got inventory."

"Sounds like a perfect storm of awful," Lilah says sympathetically.

"Pretty much," I reply, sipping my coffee. "God, that's good," I moan.

"Can you sit for a second?" Olive asks, grabbing my elbow and steering me towards their table. "I need your opinion." She's too excited to argue with, so I let her drag me over to the empty chair. Lilah pushes a binder in front of me.

"This is Olive's wedding binder," she says with a smirk.

"NO! This is my wedding planner's binder. She's the insane one, not me."

"This is the lady Chelsea used, right?" I ask.

"Yeah. And she's nuts. I've never met such a tight-ass type A personality in all my life."

"So why are you working with her?" I laugh. Two minutes with them and I already feel better.

"Because she's amazing. Chelsea's wedding was the best party I've ever been to, and I want a blowout. Plus, she did such a good job keeping everyone in line. When I met her, I thought she was a border collie. You know, herding people along, keeping a tight ship. I was wrong. She's a mother fucking pit bull. A rabid one. You should have heard her go after Joanne at the flower shop. I had to yank the phone out of her hands so she didn't make her cry."

"Pit bulls are a widely misunderstood breed," I interject.

"A wolverine? Can I call her that?"

"Go for it. Those are nightmare fuel as far as I'm concerned," I say with a grin.

"Fine, I retract the pit bull comment and substitute a rabid wolverine," Olive says. "Moving on, what do you think of these dresses?" she asks, tapping the open binder.

There are a dozen different styles, all in navy blue.

"Um… They're all pretty," I tell her.

"Lilah likes this one," Olive says, pointing to an off-the-shoulder knee-length gown with a floaty looking skirt and an empire waist. "And that should still fit perfectly in fall," she adds slyly.

Lilah gives her a look that would turn most people to stone.

"Please, you're not fooling anyone with your seltzer," Olive laughs.

I press my lips together to hide a grin and look at the ceiling. "I have no idea what she's talking about. I hadn't noticed a single thing…"

"Moving on," Lilah says, pointedly looking at the binder again.

Olive rolls her eyes at her sister, but her smile is huge when she points to a soft, gauzy looking dress with a sweetheart neckline. "I think this one would look perfect on you," she says.

My stomach drops, closely followed by my heart and lungs. "But those are bridesmaid dresses," I say quietly.

"Yes, they are, Parker," Olive says with deliberate and sarcastic slowness. "And I want you to be one of the bridesmaids. Obviously." She shakes her head, looking at me like I'm crazy for not assuming she'd want me in her wedding.

I'm the worst. The actual worst. I slept with her brother like six hours ago and then ran out on him. And I can't tell her. I can't tell any of them, but I can't keep this secret either. I swear, I thought I was all cried out before I left home this morning, but tears are pricking at the corners of my eyes again. I have to pretend like my night with Lukas never happened. I can do this. I can.

I swallow the lump in my throat and force a watery smile. "Are you sure? That's huge…"

"I'm sure!" Olive pulls me in for a tight hug. I hug her back, but I feel like an absolute rat.

18

LUKAS

I roll over and wrap my arm around Parker, still half asleep. It takes me a second to realize that she feels all squishy and another second to realize that's not Parker at all. My eyes shoot open and I sit up straight. I'm holding a pillow and there's an empty space where I expected to find Parker.

I run my hands through my hair, listening for her in the bathroom, but the house is dead silent. My heart drops because I already know she's gone. I jump out of bed and search the house to be sure. Her purse is gone and her clothes aren't in the dryer. Her bra is still hanging by the garage door, though. Great. So she bolted into the night, braless and went god knows where. How? It's not like I was keeping her hostage, but she didn't have a car. My truck is still in the garage, so she must have called someone.

Why would she do this? I don't understand. Last night was perfect. She was happy when we went to bed. Who would she call? One of my sisters, maybe?

I start to text Julia but call instead. I don't feel like waiting for a response, all things considered. She answers on the third ring.

"This had better be good," she says with a grumpy sounding groan.

"Have you seen Parker this morning?" I ask, ignoring the greeting.

"No… is there a specific reason you're worried about her whereabouts at the literal crack of dawn?"

"Can you give me her number?"

Julia makes a growly sound in her throat. "Yes, but don't tell her you got it from me, especially if you did something to piss her off."

"Deal. Text it to me." I hang up before she can say anything else. She sends the number a second later and I call it as soon as it comes through. I glance at the clock as it rings. 6:32 A.M. Where the hell would she be? Home would be the obvious answer, but I don't have her home address.

I should have made her fill out all her contact info at the garage yesterday. At least then I'd have an idea of where she'd be, but I'm a dumbass who forgot all about protocol. I was too busy watching her ass in those damn jeans to think about paperwork.

Parker doesn't answer, and I get a message that her voicemail isn't set up. I lean my elbows on the kitchen counter and run both hands through my hair as I stare at the phone, weighing my options. Worry for Parker overwhelms any concern I have about involving my other sisters, so I pull up a text with Olive and Lilah.

Me: Anyone seen Parker this morning?

Olive: Yup. She's at the bookstore early today. Inventory.

Lilah: Why do you want to know?

Me: Car stuff. Thanks.

I can feel my phone vibrating with more text messages even as I pop it in my pocket, but I ignore them. Snatching my truck keys and Parker's bra, I run out the door to my truck. I'm parked in front of her bookstore four minutes later. I can see her through the window, sitting in one of the leather armchairs. She's holding a cup of coffee in one hand. Her cheek resting on the other fist. Her eyes are closed and she looks miserable. What did I do? There's a sick, wrenching feeling in my chest that makes it hard to breathe.

I step out of the truck and walk to the front door, testing the handle. It's locked, so I rap my knuckles on the glass. Parker doesn't move, just calls out, "We're still closed." Her voice is muffled but still easy enough to hear.

I knock again and hold her bra up in the other hand. "I can come back later, but I thought you might want this."

Parker's head shoots up, her pretty blue eyes wide as saucers as she stares at me. She stands and the sight of her in that cherry print sun dress is torture, especially now that I know exactly what she looks like out of it. She stands on the other side of the door but doesn't unlock it.

"What are you doing here?" she asks.

"I would think the answer is pretty obvious," I say, swinging the bra from one finger so that it sways back and forth. "I woke up to an empty bed, no note, and no idea where you'd run off to."

Parker crosses her arms over her chest and stares at her feet. "I had to get to work."

"You don't open for another two hours." I tap the glass door between us where the hours are posted in shiny gold lettering. "Open the door."

"No. I have inventory to do."

"I call bullshit, Freckles. I don't know what I did to upset you, but I sure as hell can't fix it out here."

"You can't talk to me like that!" She shoots back and I catch a glimpse of fire in her eyes even as pink spreads across her cheeks. Good. I'll take anger over walled-off any day.

"Oh, I don't know. I think I'm allowed to be a little mad after you ran off like that with no explanation."

"Explanation?!" she yells. "Are you kidding me? Fine. Whatever! I got swept up in it, ok?! I thought last night was more than what it really was. I didn't realize that you'd want to keep it a secret, and once it dawned on me how stupid I was being, I couldn't stay. I couldn't stick around for an awkward morning when you were already ashamed of sleeping with me!"

She unlocks the door and tries to snatch her bra out of my hand, but I don't let it go. The scent of her peach shampoo washes over me and I'm hit full force with her fiery temper. I wedge my body in the door before she can slam it in my face.

"Parker, stop. You really thought I was ashamed of sleeping with you?"

She stops pulling on the bra and straightens her shoulders, her eyebrows drawing together. "You said—"

"Jesus, Freckles. I just wanted to keep you to myself for a bit. My sisters are nosy as fuck and everyone has an opinion about everything. I wanted a chance to show you how good this could be before they got involved."

Parker leans sideways, looking over my shoulder. She presses her lips together as she looks back at me, a tiny smile pulling at the edges of her face. My sisters are watching from across the street. I just know it.

"How many of them?" I ask.

"All three," she answers sheepishly.

Closing my eyes, I nod. "That sounds about right." I let go of the bra and hold her face in both hands so she's looking into my eyes. I need her to hear this.

"Listen Parker, I want to be with you and as long as you can take the crazy of my family, I don't care who knows. You weren't making last night into more than it was. The entire night with you was incredible. And I don't just mean the sex even though that was... Jesus."

Parker blushes more deeply, the color rising in her cheeks as I step closer and lean down to whisper in her ear.

"I barely got a taste of you last night." Stroking my fingers down the sides of her throat, I bite her earlobe, enjoying the way she shivers and leans into my touch. "And if you think I'd let you go that easily, I'll have to show you how persistent I can be. Tell me you want more, Parker. Say yes," I growl quietly.

Parker makes a little whimpering sound in the back of her throat and grabs a fistful of my shirt. "Ok. I mean, yes. Just come inside," she says breathlessly.

"Yes ma'am," I say with a smirk, letting her pull me across the threshold. Slipping my hand into her hair, I grip the back of her neck and kiss her. Her lips part for me, her tongue teasing mine. Blood roars in my ears as I slam the door behind me, turning the lock. I steer her to the back corner of the shop, hidden behind a bookshelf and out of sight of the windows. Gathering Parker's wrists in one hand, I lift them over her head, pinning her to the wall. She arches her back, her breasts making a bid for freedom from the cherry sundress.

Parker's kisses turn frantic, her breathing shallow pants. "I'm sorry I ran off," she says, her lips brushing mine. "I'm so sorry, you just— you hit a nerve when you said you wanted to keep it a secret. I couldn't face you."

"Shh… it's ok, baby. But if you run off again, I'm going to spank your ass. You know that, right?" I say, pressing a thigh between her legs and slipping a hand under the skirt of her dress to give her ass a little smack. I'm expecting the yelp of surprise, but the way she moans and grinds on my thigh sets my blood on fire.

"Fuck, you're so hot," I growl, holding her jaw in my hand so I can watch the desire flair in her eyes. "I love it when you grind on me like that. You like it when I'm rough with you?"

Parker's eyes light up and she nods.

"Say it, baby. I like it when those sweet little lips ask for filthy things."

She licks her lips, her breath coming in excited pants. "I like it when you're rough," she breathes.

"You like it when I'm in charge?" I lower myself to whisper in her ear, slipping a finger under the waistband of her panties and running it around her hip before snapping it softly.

"Yes!" she gasps, grinding on my thigh harder.

"Good, because you make me fucking crazy, Parker, and I don't want to hold back."

"Then don't," she pants, rolling her hips against me again. Slipping my hand under her panties, I dip a finger into her folds. A feral sound rips its way out of my throat. She's not just wet for me. She's slippery and hot when my fingers spread her lips, her clit a swollen bud just begging to be stroked. My cock is throbbing in my jeans, desperate to sink into her warmth. I run my fingers around the edges of that little pearl. Parker is panting with need, squirming on my thigh.

"You need more?" I ask, biting my way down her neck.

"Yes," she whimpers.

"Is that sweet little pussy empty and aching for me?" I gently grasp the sides of her bud, loving her gasping moan for more.

"I'm going to bend you over, pull those soaking wet panties to the side, and fuck you until you can't stand anymore. Is that what you want?"

Rolling my fingers around her clit elicits a wailing, "Yes, oh my God. Yes!"

"Good girl," I growl, pulling my hand out of her panties and releasing her wrists. Spinning her around so her hands hit the wall, I run my hand down her spine, admiring the curve of her hips before gripping them and pulling her ass towards me. Her back arches, giving me what I want. I'm shaking with need. I can hear my pulse in my ears, pounding so hard it's deafening. It's torture not being inside her.

Running a hand up the back of her thighs, I grasp the hem of her dress, tossing it up over her back. White cotton panties cover her heart-shaped ass, and it's all I can do not to bite through my lip. I rub a hand over her backside. The lights are off but the morning light is filtering through the bookshop windows and it's just enough to appreciate the way she's soaked through those innocent-looking panties.

She's so angelic and it makes me feel irreverent in the best way.

"Spread your legs for me, Freckles," I order with a smirk. Parker looks at me over her shoulder, eyes filled with lust as she does what I say. She watches as I unbuckle my belt and unzip my jeans, moaning when I free my cock, stroking it in my fist. I give her ass a quick smack before meeting her eyes again. Her eyes are glazed, her pouty lips parted in surprise.

"You going to run off on me again, Parker?" I ask, pulling my wallet out of my back pocket and retrieving a condom.

"Will you spank me again if I say yes?" she asks, her face full of false innocence.

I open the condom and roll it on with ruthless efficiency before leaning over her back. My hard cock presses against her backside, aching as I kiss her and wrap her strawberry curls in my fist.

"Yes," I say against her lips.

"Then yes," she whispers back with a coquettish smile. I feel the smirk spread across my face as my dick throbs against her ass. I think I fucking love her.

Standing straight, I keep hold of her hair as I pull her panties down her legs. I let her step out of them before smacking her other ass cheek. Parker jumps a little, moaning when I run my fingers over the swell of flesh where I can see a faint handprint appearing on her pale skin.

"What about now?" I ask, dipping a finger into her glistening pink folds. "You going to run off again?"

"Yes," she moans, quivering in anticipation.

I put my finger in my mouth, sucking her honey off it before landing a quick swat on each of her ass cheeks.

"Oh my God…" she moans.

I press the head of my cock to her entrance, rubbing it against her. "How about now, Freckles? You going to run off on me again now?" She's so turned on that she's squirming against me, her pussy swollen and pink with need. "If you promise to be good, I can give you this cock. That's what you want, isn't it? You want me to fill you up and make you come." I push inside her just a fraction of an inch. It's killing me not to sink balls deep, but I love the way she's writhing.

"I promise!" she gasps. She presses back, but I grab her hip and don't let her get any extra.

"Whose girl are you?" I ask, tightening my grip on her hip as she squirms.

"Yours! I'm yours!"

A possessive surge of pleasure ripples through me. "Good girl. Now tell me what you want, Parker."

"I want you to fuck me!" she cries out.

I plunge into her, pulling on her ponytail for leverage. Her sweet hot pussy grasps me, squeezing me like a fist. She feels so fucking good. I can't see straight.

"Oh my God, yes!" she screams into the wall. I hope no one is in the shop next door because she is definitely not quiet.

"Fuck, that's so good," I groan. "You're so goddamn tight." My voice is gravel as I tunnel in and out of her. Letting go of her ponytail, I reach around, pressing my fingers in a V around her clit, stroking in time with my thrusts.

Parker moans, "Put your hand on my neck."

"Dirty girl," I grit out. I'm so worked up, I can't last. It feels too good. Wrapping an arm around her chest, I grip the sides of her neck, careful to avoid her windpipe as I hold her in place, fucking her hard.

Her legs start to shake, and she grips my thigh with her nails. "Yes. Oh God. Yes, like that—"

I try to focus on something besides how fucking good she feels wrapped around my cock. Anything to distract me long enough to make her come first, but she's so tight... and I'm losing it.

Parker's body tenses, trembling violently, and she cries my name into the quiet of the shop, her pussy clenching around me like a vice. It robs me of my last vestiges of control, ripping me apart as I empty myself inside her.

"Oh my God," Parker lets out a low chuckle, her body sandwiched between me and the wall. Releasing her neck and pulling out, I turn her around carefully so I can kiss her. The panic and anger I've been feeling all morning is gone. All I want to do now is hold her. She lets me wrap her up in my arms, her soft curves melting into me as she wraps her arms around my waist and rubs her hands over my back. She kisses me so sweetly, so full of affection that it makes my heart twist. I love this.

My phone buzzes and I know it's probably Asher wondering where I am. I should be at the auto shop by now, but I can't find it in me to care.

"Stay with me tonight?" I ask, my lips brushing against Parker's.

"You'll have to pick me up," she grins. "My mechanic is the worst."

I give her a shocked look. "He's the best. He's just had *much* better things to do."

Parker laughs, her eyes shining as she looks down at my situation. "It's not very professional for him to have his dick out in front of a client, though."

"You're right," I say, feigning chagrin. "Almost as unprofessional as nailing a client in the back of your bookshop." I make a *tsk*ing sound through my teeth and shake my head at her.

She laughs again and peeks around the edge of the bookshelf. "Fine, you win. We're both terrible. Go clean up," she says, pushing me towards the bathroom.

By the time I get cleaned up, Parker is straightening things behind the counter. She looks tired but happy. I set my truck keys on the counter.

"Use my truck until I get your Civic fixed, ok?"

"I can't—" she argues, but I kiss her, pulling her against me.

"You can and you will," I insist, kissing down her neck and giving her a soft bite. She shivers and giggles, pushing me away.

"Stop, you're going to turn me on again."

"Fine," I sigh dejectedly as I step out from behind the counter, sliding the keys towards the register. "Pack an overnight bag and pick me up at the shop when you're done tonight."

"You just get to decide we're having a sleepover? Don't I get a say?" she teases.

"Hell no. I was robbed. I didn't get to wake up to you this morning. You're going to park that fine ass in my bed all night long so I can treat you right in the morning," I say, wiggling my eyebrows at her.

"Bossy," Parker says, grinning as she leans over the counter to kiss me goodbye. The way she's leaning forward gives me a view of her cleavage that would probably kill a man with a weak heart. I groan, copping a quick feel as I take the offered kiss and grinning when she swats my hand.

It's a quick walk to the auto shop and I stroll in, whistling and feeling lighter than air. Asher is his usual grumpy self as I pass his office door. He's shuffling papers on his desk, scowling at the order forms.

"You're late," he says without looking up. "You get to work through lunch."

I keep moving and call out over my shoulder, "Worth it."

19

PARKER

I try to put myself back together after Lukas leaves, but it's a losing battle. I look awful from my long, sleepless night and thoroughly rumpled from our tryst behind the stacks. My ponytail is in a sad state after being grabbed with rough, sexy hands, so I take it down and then wrap my hair in a messy bun. I keep trying to smooth the wrinkles out of my dress, but it's beyond saving.

It's quiet at the bookshop all morning, but my heart keeps fluttering, my blood rushing every time I think about Lukas. It's nearly impossible to keep my mind on anything else for more than a minute at a time.

I wish more than once I could make a cup of tea, kicking myself for not bringing my mug from home. I'm trying to work up the courage to cross the street and get a cup of coffee from Olive, but I'm not sure I can face Lukas' sisters yet. The looks on their faces when Lukas confronted me were, well… yikes.

Olive appeared surprised, but she had an arm out, holding back a livid, emotional Lilah. Julia was wearing her trademark smirk. And I can only imagine what they must think of me after I pulled him inside like that.

My stomach starts rumbling around noon. I haven't eaten

anything since the tacos last night, and right now I'm running on a single cup of coffee. I feel sick from lack of sleep and what I suspect is an adrenaline crash from my blowup and subsequent make-up with Lukas. I wrap my arms around my stomach, trying to forget my hunger for the time being, and put my head down on the counter.

The bell over the door chimes and I jolt upright. I don't know how long I was asleep, but there is drool at the corner of my mouth that I try to wipe away discreetly while focusing on the figure coming in the door.

"Don't bother trying to be sneaky. We could see you passed out from across the street," Julia says, eyes sparkling with affectionate humor. "You've got a post-it stuck to your forehead, by the way."

"Oh. Um… thanks." Sheepishly, I remove the post-it and check to see if it's anything important before tossing it in the trash. Olive and Lilah follow Julia inside, carrying brown paper bags and cups of coffee. Lilah hip-bumps the door, shutting it with a flourish.

"What are you guys doing?" I ask as they head to the couches and start pulling food out of the bags.

"We brought you lunch," Lilah says. I think she sounds a little stiff, but she smiles at me just the same.

"And we had to check that you were still alive after the way you yanked Lukas in here this morning," Julia adds with a smirk.

Olive elbows her in the side, "Ew. Stop."

Julia shrugs, sipping her coffee and holding a travel cup out for me. I walk around the counter and take the offered cup. "Maybe it's the nurse training, but I'm ok separating the fact that Lukas is our brother from the fact that Parker is *finally* getting deep-dicked like she deserves."

Lilah chokes on her drink and Olive cackles as I blush so hard my face burns. Julia grins at me, patting the sofa next to her before grabbing my arm and pulling me down next to her when I don't move fast enough.

"We talked about this before coming over," she says, looking at her sisters as if to remind them, just as much to reassure me. "You're our girl, Parker. No matter what."

Olive nods and hands me a sandwich. "Julia is right. This changes nothing between us. Except, please don't give me details. I'll puke."

"Deal," I laugh, blinking back the grateful tears that are threatening to spill. "I'm sorry. I really wanted to tell you this morning, but things were weird between Lukas and me. We... had a misunderstanding."

"And made up, from the looks of it," Julia says, wiggling her eyebrows at me, making me laugh harder even as Olive pretends to gag.

Lilah sets down her coffee and opens her mouth like she wants to say something but purses her lips instead. I can tell that she's not on board with this like her sisters and honestly, that really sucks. She and I have been close since the first day we met. She is the person I reach out to most often, the sister who seemed to get me the most.

"You might as well say whatever you're thinking," I tell her. "If you're mad at me, I get it. If you don't want me dating Lukas, I understand." It won't change my mind, but I don't say that part out loud because it most certainly wouldn't be helpful right now.

Lilah's eyes widen with surprise and then narrow into an irritated expression. "It's not you, Parker! For God's sake. You can date anyone you want, family or otherwise, and I'll be happy for you."

I shake my head in confusion. "Then what—?"

"It's Lukas!" Lilah interrupts. "You're so sweet and he's... well. He's my brother, so I love him, but I don't want to see you get hurt." She looks at her sisters, appealing for them to see her side of it. "Does nobody remember what happened with Sadie?"

"Ok, but counterpoint, Sadie was the worst," Julia argues.

"The total worst," Olive confirms.

"But Lukas was *terrible* to her. It ruined our friendship and he really hurt her—"

My blood started heating the second Lilah brought up Sadie's name. I told her I would understand, but that was when I thought she was suspicious of me, not him. And I can't let her sit there, thinking the worst of him. I don't know everything about his past, but I know enough to defend him. And even if he doesn't think it's worth bringing up, I do.

"Stop it," I say firmly.

Lilah looks at me, shocked. Even Olive and Julia appear taken aback. Three sets of matching green eyes stare at me like I've just announced that I enjoy eating puppies with a side of kitten. To be fair, I've never spoken like that in front of them. Or anyone really, except for Lukas. But at least I have their attention.

"For one thing, Lukas and I already talked about Sadie. If you only have her side, then you don't have the whole story. Full disclosure, you might not *want* all the details," I say, making an awkward face. Julia laughs next to me as I continue, building a head of steam. "Second, I might come from a small town and maybe I seem sweet and a little too innocent, but I'm not. I can handle my shit and I can sure as hell handle Lukas and whatever he did in the past," I finish, a little breathless, but still firm and rather proud of myself.

Julia applauds and hugs my head. "Yay! That's my girl," she says before releasing me. Lilah gives me a half-smile and shrugs one shoulder.

"Maybe I've been a little overprotective of you. I can... get that way."

Olive laughs, "It's true. She threatened Brooks with a knife once."

"I did not! That was Luis," Lilah argues, looking up toward the ceiling as she tries to remember the specifics. "I think I just threatened to bury him in a shallow grave if he hurt you. Weapons were implied but not present for that one. I'm sorry, Parker. I can ease up."

"Thank you. I love that you're worried about me. I really do."

Lilah reaches out and squeezes my hand, and my heart aches with happiness. How did I get so lucky with my friends? Sonoma would be a very different, very lonely place without them.

"I got new books in yesterday, do you want to see?" I ask.

Olive squeals through a mouthful of sandwich and just like that, things feel almost normal again.

The girls hang out for almost an hour, passing around the new books and gossiping before Julia announces that she has to head to work.

"How's it going with that doctor?" Olive asks her.

"What?" I gasp. "Are you dating a doctor? How did we not talk about this?"

Julia shrugs, looking bored. "I'm not. He asked, and I went to dinner with him once, but I'm really not interested. He's certainly not worth bringing to family dinner."

Olive gasps, her face lighting up with excitement as she smacks my arm.

"Ow! What—?"

"Family dinner," she grins. "You have to come now."

I think my blood pressure drops so low I could pass out. "I don't know. Lukas didn't bring it up and—"

"He will," she says confidently. "And Gran will be thrilled."

Lilah pokes Olive in the side. "You just want a buffer so Gran will stop asking when you're going to pop out a baby."

"Funny, you'd think someone else might speak up and save me from the Spanish Inquisition on that one," Olive says, staring daggers at Lilah's midsection.

"I have no idea what you're talking about," Lilah says before running out the door. "Nice try, Decaf!" Olive yells, shaking Lilah's empty coffee cup at her back as she hustles across the street.

"I swear to god, she's not fooling anyone," Olive mutters, collecting the trash in one of the bags.

"Don't be salty," Julia chides. "This is perfect. The second she tells Gran, you and I are in the clear. That baby is going to buy us *years* of peace."

"Months, at best," Olive retorts with a snort. "We need a better distraction."

"Oh, I have an idea," I say to Julia. "Bring that doctor to your family dinner and pass him off to your gran. She'd enjoy getting handsy with the fresh meat, and I bet he'd stop hounding you. Win-win."

Julia cackles, holding the door for Olive. "This is why I love you. You're a little wicked under that cotton candy exterior." She winks as she closes the door behind her.

"See you at dinner on Friday, Parker!" Olive calls as she crosses the street back to the bakery.

Friday? Crap. My birthday is on Friday. I haven't told anyone, but maybe I should? They might feel bad if I spend the evening with them and don't say anything, even if it's just because I'm shy about my birthday. Maybe Lukas won't bring up dinner and I can just spend a quiet night at home.

The store picks up after my lunch with the girls. A steady stream of tourists, fresh off their winery tours, keeps me on my feet. A trio of drunk women in pearls and polos asks me to pull the raunchiest books I can think of. They buy everything I put in front of them, hanging out until closing time, flipping through their purchases, and comparing notes on the dirtiest bits. I pretend not to notice the poorly concealed baby-pink flasks they keep drinking from.

I shoo them out the door one minute after closing time, pointing them in the right direction of their hotel before locking the door and flipping the closed sign. I'm dead on my feet and skip a lot of my usual dusting and straightening. I can do it in the morning.

I grab my purse, which is finally dry, and check my phone. I have half a dozen questions from Olive about bridesmaid dresses and measurements, but I scroll down to the one text message from Lukas from three o'clock this afternoon.

Lukas: Thinking about you, Freckles.

I'm smiling so hard my cheeks hurt as I respond.

Me: Sorry, I just got this. Busy day. I just locked up and need to go grab some clothes. I was thinking about you too.

My feet hit the sidewalk and for a second I worry that I should have asked Lukas where he parked his truck, but as soon as I hit the unlock button on the key fob, I laugh. Turns out, it's hard to miss. The massive, shiny black truck is parked one store down, practically blocking out the sun.

Shaking my head, I open the driver's side door and climb in. Literally. I have to grab the back of the seat and jump up into the dang thing. I'd say he was compensating for something, but I know for a fact that's not true.

It's a puzzle getting the seat in the right position with the little power-adjust buttons, but I get it scooted forward and lifted high enough so I can see out the windshield. I feel guilty messing with all the mirrors, knowing that Lukas will just have to fix them later.

Cujo isn't at the gate when I get home, but I pull out the sandwich crusts I saved for him and toss them over the fence, anyway. At least that way he'll know I brought him something.

It's almost comical, packing an overnight bag from my meager possessions in the tiny house. By the time I pull out a couple changes of clothes, my toiletries, and toothbrush, there's almost nothing left. I pop my mug in my bag so I can take it to work with me tomorrow. At the last minute, I go back into my drawer and pack extra panties. Can't be too safe when I'm going to be sharing space with Lukas.

I'm giddy at the thought of seeing him again and practically skip to the truck. The last two days have been emotional whiplash, but I'm on a high right now and I'm happy to roll with it.

Asher is in front of the Donovan Auto when I pull in fifteen minutes later. He raises an eyebrow, giving me a little salute. I swear the entire family is such a matching set. It's not just the eyes, though the bright green is certainly a family trademark. They've all mastered the single cocked eyebrow that perfectly conveys "well-well-well-what-have-we-here?" and the "I'm-smirking-on-the-inside" lip press. Asher gives me both as I climb out of the truck.

"What did you do?" he asks.

"Do? I don't think I did anything..." I trail off, confused. I turn to look at the truck, making sure I didn't scratch it accidentally. It still looks perfect...

"Not talking about the truck," Asher says.

"Well, you're being kind of cryptic," I answer. I don't know where the Donovan cloth is, but the trimmings are out there somewhere with Asher's shape cut out right next to Lukas' outline.

"He's whistling. It's annoying." Asher jerks his head towards the auto bay where I can see Lukas moving around my Civic, faint notes of cheerful whistling filtering across the lot. My chest tightens in a happy squeeze.

"Sorry." I grin back at Asher, not missing the eye roll. Another Donovan trait, I think. "I'll see what I can do."

I leave my stuff in the truck cab and cross the lot. Heat is rising off the blacktop in shimmering waves. Lukas has his back to me as I approach. I can't tell what song he's whistling, but the romantic side of me loves that I make him so happy.

My inner dirty girl doesn't give a flying fuck about the whistling. She's way too distracted by the view. He has the top half of his mechanic coverall things undone and tied around his waist, showing off his thoroughly bitable butt.

There are grease stains on the back of his white tank top and technically, I know that shouldn't be sexy... I thought I was firmly in the No Man-Tank camp, but boy was I *wrong*. The muscles in Lukas' broad shoulders are exposed, tattoos rippling as he works on something at a beat-up workbench. He's dirty and sweaty, and when he wipes his forehead with a rag and shoves it in his back pocket, I nearly lose my head entirely.

I'm starting to feel like a creeper, so I hold up his keys, jingling them to announce my presence. Lukas turns and gives me a huge, breathtaking grin. He has a dark smudge on one cheek and it just makes him even more irresistible.

"Hey Freckles," he says, eyes sweeping over my body appreciatively as I step closer.

"For the record, the whole dirty mechanic thing is really working for me," I tell him, gesturing to all of him with a finger.

"Oh, yeah?" he asks, setting down a wrench and a car part on the bench.

I suck my lower lip between my teeth, biting it and nodding. "Oh yeah," I tell him, brushing his hair out of his face. He smells manly but there's that familiar laundry detergent underneath the engine oil and sweat and it makes me think about curling up in his sheets, tucked against his side.

Lukas puts his mouth next to my ear and speaks quietly. "I can't touch you like this though. I'd get you all dirty."

I shiver despite the heat. I *love* it when he does that. There's something so... illicit about the feel of his breath on my neck and the low rumble of his voice next to my ear. Maybe it's the fact that those words are just for me.

"I'm pretty sure that ship has sailed," I whisper back. "You've already gotten me dirty once today. Twice last night." I bite his earlobe gently.

"You're killing me, Freckles," he groans as I step back and smile sweetly at him.

"What's the damage on my Civic?" I ask with a wince. It's hard to ignore the fact that it's torn apart. The engine has been pulled out and parts of it are staged around the workbench. It looks organized, but in a way that is completely foreign to me.

"It's coming along," Lukas says, turning his attention back to the part he's cleaning with a greasy rag. "It's too hot out here. Get your sexy ass in my office while I clean up. There's cold water in the fridge."

"Bossy." I grin at him before heading inside. I steal a bottle of cold water and settle in to read in his office. I only get a few pages in when my phone rings with an unfamiliar number.

"Hello?"

"Hi, is this Parker Thompson from Sorry, I'm Booked?"

"Yes," I hedge, confused. Why does this woman have my cell number instead of the shop one?

"Hi Miss Thompson," she continues cheerily. "My name is Ashley; your friend Sally gave me your number. I'm Mackenna Jade's personal assistant. I'm assuming you're familiar with her romance novels?"

I nearly swallow my tongue in excitement. "Yes, I'm familiar," the words squeak out of me in a decidedly fan-girl manner. To be fair, her Riding Dirty series was my very first introduction to the world of possessive ranch hands and cowboys.

"Fabulous. I'm looking for independent bookstores willing to host Ms. Jade for book signings. After talking to Sally, I thought your shop might be a good fit."

My brain is on the verge of exploding. This would be huge. Like national attention huge.

"Oh my God, yes! That would be amazing," I choke out. "She can have any day, any time she wants!"

"Great," Ashley laughs a little at my enthusiasm. "Let me give you my contact info and we can talk in the next week or so to schedule a date."

"Hang on, let me find a pen and some paper." I reach for my

purse, but I left it in the car. Of course, I did. Springing to my feet, I round Lukas' desk and open the top drawer, pulling out a notebook as I reach for one of the pens lying on the desk.

I flip through the pages looking for a blank one, but immediately realize it's not a notebook. It's a sketchbook. It falls open to a pencil drawing of the beach; the surf crashing on the shore in breathtaking accuracy while little sandpipers run through the sand. The date at the bottom is from today with the words "Parker/ Kehoe."

I turn back a page and suck in a breath. A manly hand rests on a woman's thigh, her skin dotted with little freckles. It's so intimate it makes my chest ache.

Flipping again, I put a hand over my mouth. The woman in the picture is unmistakably me. I'm looking down at my hands, smiling softly, my hair falling in wild curls over one shoulder of his black t-shirt.

There are more. One of me dancing in a faceless crowd in the outfit I wore to Sally's party, dated the day before last. One of me in the same cherry print dress I'm wearing today, reaching for a book on a shelf.

There's one dated the night of my last book club. Lukas drew me standing on the far side of my bookshop. Blurry shadows fill the edges of the paper, but my figure is crystal clear, staring straight out of the page, mouth parted, eyes full of wonder and lust. I look beautiful. Ethereal.

The memory of the moment hits me, the physical manifestation of those emotions filling my body all over again. I wanted him so badly, was drawn to him so strongly, that it defied reason. And somehow, he captured every ounce of that in this one beautiful sketch. My heart is pounding in my chest, my ribs being pulled in every direction at once.

"Hello? Are you still there?"

Oh my god. Right. The phone. "Yeah, sorry. I uh... I got distracted for a second. I'm ready now," I say, grabbing a torn envelope from the desk. I copy down her info, promising to call in the morning so we can confirm a date.

Under any other circumstances, I'd be flying high after that phone call, but I almost don't even care that a best-selling author is going to do a signing in my little store. I just want to get her off the phone so I can focus on these sketches.

Ashley finally hangs up and I slide my phone back into my pocket before dropping into Lukas' desk chair. Scanning through the pages, I realize the dates on the other sketches are farther apart. Before me, he was drawing one or two a month at most. There's a nice one of his sisters sitting near a fire pit and one of his gran baking something in an apron from last Christmas. Most of the sketches are little daily things, all beautiful in their simplicity.

Maybe I'm vain, but all I want to look at are the sketches he drew of me. I love imagining each stroke of his pencil scraping along the paper as he thought of me. How he did these from memory, I'll never understand, but it's clear from the way he captures the emotion that he sees more than he lets on, banking it away quietly.

"I should know better than to leave you alone in here by now."

I whip my gaze up to Lukas, leaning in the door frame. He's cleaned himself up and is drying his hands with a paper towel. A wave of cold guilt hits me hard and fast. This was in his drawer. It was private. If he wanted to show it to me, he would have, but now it looks like I went snooping through his things.

20

LUKAS

Watching Parker swing her hips as she goes inside, knowing that I can't even touch her, is a special kind of torture. As soon as she's out of sight, I drop the drive plate on the workbench with a sigh.

The engine on the Civic is completely shot. The drive plate is cracked, the seals are basically crumbling, and worst of all, the bearings are toast. There's so much metal shaved off in her oil that I'm actually surprised the radiator went first.

The car is unfixable. It would cost at least twice what the Civic is worth to repair the damn thing. Factoring in the age and overall shittiness of the car, rolling it off a cliff for the $10 insurance payout would be the most financially sound outcome.

I should tell her the truth, but I know Parker can't afford a new car. It's going to ruin her day and stress her out. And selfishly, I don't want to do that right now. I could just buy her a new one, courtesy of my trust fund, but we're two days into a relationship and that feels... excessive. I know she wants to stand on her own two feet, but I'm going to have to convince her to let me help because I don't think I'm capable of standing by and watching her struggle.

At the moment, the only plan I can come up with is having Parker keep my truck while I "work" on her car. Asher won't like it sitting in the bay, taking up space, but at least it will buy me some time to come up with a better plan.

I'm still mulling it over in my head, cleaning up as best as I can. Getting all the stains off my hands is a losing battle, even with the industrial-strength hand scrub we keep around, but at least I'll be able to grab Parker by the hips and pull her close without ruining her clothes.

You've already gotten me dirty once today.

Just thinking about her whispering those words has me adjusting myself. I feel like I keep peeling back layers of Parker to find dirtier, sexier layers underneath, and I fucking love that no one but me would even suspect it. I want to take her out for dinner, but first I'm going to put her ass on my desk and eat her pussy until she screams.

I'm just about to leave the bathroom when my phone rings in my pocket. "Fuck," I mutter when I see Lilah's name on the caller ID. I could screen the call, but I know she won't let up. I might as well get it over with.

"Hey," I answer warily. "Am I about to get my ass chewed out? Just trying to prepare myself."

"No…" Lilah trails off. "Parker doesn't need me to protect her from you. She's a grownup."

She pauses and I wait, unwilling to say anything that's going to piss her off. I am intimately aware of how grown-up Parker is, but saying so would push Lilah's buttons in the worst way.

"Do I know the entire story with you and Sadie?" she asks abruptly. I'm not sure what I expected, but it sure as hell wasn't that.

"No," I answer truthfully, but god help me, I don't want to share the specifics with my sisters.

"Do I want to know the whole story?"

"Probably not," I hedge. "Why are you asking about this?"

Lilah laughs awkwardly. "Olive, Julia, and I had lunch with Parker today."

I grind my teeth and swear softly.

"We wanted to make sure she knew we were still here for her. You made this really awkward, you know that?"

"It's none of your business," I grit out.

"Oh, I'm aware!" Lilah laughs. "Parker made it pretty clear that she can handle her own shit, which I love by the way. She also pointed out that maybe I haven't had the whole picture when it comes to you. And if that's true, I just thought… maybe I haven't been totally fair either."

I'm speechless. I can't believe she stood up for me like that. To Lilah, of all people.

"It's fine," I tell her.

"Well… I'm sorry, anyway. She really likes you, you know," she says.

"What did she say?" I ask, peeking around the corner of the bathroom door. I can see Parker's shadow moving in my office.

Lilah laughs, "Not much. And I'm not breaking girl code. I just thought you should know."

I know I've got a stupid-looking grin on my face when I step into my office, but it freezes when I see Parker sitting behind my desk with my sketchbook open in front of her. Blood pounds in my ears, panic rising in my chest. How could I have left that lying around for her to find? My gut reaction is to snatch it away, afraid that she's going to freak out when she sees what I've drawn. I've never shown those to anyone and I'm well aware how fucking stalkery it looks to have a bunch of sketches of her from before we were even dating.

The only thing that stops me from grabbing it and tossing it out the window is the admiration on Parker's face. She's staring at the sketch I drew this afternoon of her wearing my shirt. In my bed. Her fingertips are pressed to her lips as her eyes glide over the paper, filled with the softest, sweetest expression I've ever seen. The panic in my chest subsides. I can't argue with that expression.

"I should know better than to leave you alone in here by now," I say.

Parker jumps, her head snapping up, eyes wide and guilty. She stares at me for a beat before slamming the notebook closed and jumping to her feet.

"I'm so sorry. Oh my God," she says, sliding it towards me. "I—I needed a piece of paper. I didn't mean— I'm so sorry, Lukas." She looks like she's about to cry and lord knows I can't take the sight of her tears.

"It's ok, Freckles." I cross the office, sitting on the edge of my desk and pulling her to stand between my legs.

"I really wasn't trying to snoop," she whispers, her eyes full of miserable apology.

"I know. It's ok. Really." My hands encircle her waist, smoothing over the swell of her hips "See anything you liked?" I ask with a raised eyebrow.

"Yes," she admits softly. "I didn't know you could draw."

I chuckle. "It's not something I share with most people. It's just a… hobby."

"But you're really good at it." Warmth curls its way through my chest at her praise. Normally I'd say I don't give a fuck what anyone thinks of me, but with Parker, I care. Her opinion matters.

"Thank you," I say, bending to kiss her neck. "Why don't we get out of here… I can get you naked and you can give me some more inspiration."

"Mmm hm," she sighs happily. She presses her hands on my thighs, pushing back. She sways a little on her feet, and I realize she has dark circles under her eyes.

"Did you sleep at all last night?" I ask, concern rising in me when she looks away.

"Not really," she says sheepishly. "But I took a nap on the counter at the store. Does that count?"

"Nope. Alright, come on then," I say. "You like Italian?" Parker nods with a sleepily looking grin. Grabbing my phone, I shoot off a quick order to my favorite place down the street before packing up my stuff. I tuck my sketchbook back in the drawer. "Look at it anytime you want. I don't mind," I say. "I just like having it at work."

Parker gives me the truck keys. She's dead on her feet and I'm already salty that she drove here that tired. I get halfway into the driver's seat when I realize I'll never fit. Stepping back out I laugh as I slide the seat back.

"Sorry!" Parker says with a blush. "Short legs."

"I like your short legs," I reply with a grin. "I just didn't know the seat went that far forward."

Parker waits in the truck while I run in and grab dinner from the little Italian restaurant. We pull into my driveway a couple minutes later and I make it around the front of the cab to open the door for her by the time she's unbuckled her seat belt. She laughs, thanking me as she jumps down. I grab her bag from the back and sling it over my shoulder. The grin she gives me as I juggle everything is worth it. Honestly, that smile would be worth it even if I had to walk across a field of Legos.

We spread the food out on my small table, eating out of the Styrofoam containers. Parker moans around every bite of the chicken parmesan, and I make a mental note to order that one for her next time.

"Where did you learn to draw like that?" Parker asks as she steals a meatball from the container in front of me.

"I just kind of figured it out," I tell her. "It was something I started doing as a kid."

"Yeah?" Parker asks, watching and waiting for me to elaborate. I shift in my seat, debating how to explain this.

"Yeah, so you know my mom passed away and my dad left us with Gran, right?"

Parker's eyebrows draw together as she nods sadly.

"Yeah. Some of us handled it better than others. I was way too young to understand, all I knew was my world had been turned upside down. I didn't know how to cope, so I was just a huge pain in the ass. My gran was patient, but she forced me to go see this shrink. I wasn't much for sharing, but one thing she asked me to do was to keep a journal. Coming up with words was too hard, so I just drew pictures of what happened around me. I did it for so long that it became a habit, and then I ended up enjoying it."

Parker watches me with admiration in her eyes, and I'm struck by the way she gives me her full attention. Her big blue eyes never leave my face. She listens intently like she wants to catch every word of what I have to say, and it makes me talk more than I'm used to. She draws things out of me like no one else has.

"Can I ask you about something in your sketches?" Parker asks, digging her fork around in her pasta. She's adorable when she's shy.

"Of course."

"There weren't any other women. I mean, besides your family." She blushes and keeps her eyes down like she's dreading what I might say.

"Well, that's less of a question and more of a statement," I tease. "I sketch the things that feel important. You feel important." I shrug. A heart-stopping smile spreads across Parker's face, lighting up her eyes as a blush spreads across her cheeks.

"But you've dated around," she argues.

"A bit, yeah. I've definitely got a reputation, but let's just say that the reports of my man-whoring have been greatly exaggerated."

Parker chokes on a sip of water. "Did you just bastardize Mark Twain in your defense of serial dating?" She laughs.

I grin at her. "Of course, you know that quote."

"Book nerd, right here," she says, pointing at her face. "I mostly read romances, but I know my literary history."

"I love that about you," I say, before clearing my throat. *Phrasing, asshat,* I think to myself. "It's just... when I fuck up, I fuck up publicly. I don't always think things through the way I should."

Parker nods. "And I overthink almost everything."

"Do me a favor," I say, leaning close. "Don't overthink this."

She grins at me. "Deal. You planning to take me to bed soon?"

———

"THIS ISN'T EXACTLY what I had in mind," she says as I tuck the blanket around her.

We put the leftovers in the fridge, and she followed me upstairs, smiling sleepily at me when I lifted her dress over her head. It took every decent bone in my body not to rip her bra off, throw her on the bed, and make her come half a dozen times. I'm not sure how I managed to find a clean t-shirt and pop it back over her head before I could give in.

She was easy enough to steer into bed but started getting suspicious when I climbed in next to her and pulled the blanket up, desperately trying to block out the mental images fighting their way to the surface. Slipping her panties down her legs, spreading her thighs, and licking her until she's screaming my name… The hot, tight clasp of her pussy, gripping my cock while I empty myself into her. My runaway thoughts are threatening to ruin my best intentions.

"I'm not an expert, but this feels like the weirdest foreplay," she says, tilting her head to the side and squinting at me.

She needs sleep, I tell myself. *She'll be here in the morning.* At least she fucking better be. Although, now that I think about it, she liked the spanking so much that she might slide out of bed just to get a repeat. I briefly wish I had a pair of handcuffs just to make sure she stays put.

"That's because it's not foreplay, it's bedtime. You're exhausted."

"I'm not *too* exhausted…" she lies, blinking slowly like her eyelids are too heavy to hold up.

"You can barely keep your eyes open, Freckles."

"I can fool around with my eyes closed," she argues.

I chuckle, pulling her body against mine, running my hand along the dip of her hip before kissing her slow and deep. Her movements are languid, and I love the way she sighs happily.

"See, totally good to go," she murmurs against my lips even as her muscles relax. It's impossible to tear my eyes away from Parker, especially like this. Her coppery curls spill over my arm and shoulder, her breath teasing my chest.

She's still for a long time, but when she stirs, it's to slide her arm over my ribs and hitch her leg over mine. I love that even in her sleep she wants to wrap herself around me.

I didn't know I was walking around with a perforated soul, but Parker is filling in all these little holes. Protecting her, taking care of her like this, it fills a piece of my soul that I didn't know was empty. It feels the same when she puts her trust in me, giving me that sweet open look that makes me feel like I can do no wrong.

I don't know if I deserve to feel this good, but one thing is for sure: no one and nothing is coming between me and Parker. They'll have to pry her from my cold, dead hands.

I always thought it was weird when I saw couples go all in, but now that I'm here, I realize there's no other option for me.

21

PARKER

I wake up slowly, so warm and comfortable it should be illegal. There's a heavy hand resting on my bare hip and as I stretch, Lukas' work-roughened fingers stroke my skin. I feel *amazing*. I haven't slept that comfortably in… well, ever.

I always wanted to be one of those independent, happy-to-be-on-my-own women. I wanted to be like Julia, free spirited and taking shit from no man. But that's not me. I'm a hopeless romantic and nothing in this world compares to the feeling of waking up in Lukas' arms; warm, safe, and adored.

His fingers stroke my hip again, tracing the top edge of my panties and pressing a kiss to the top of my head.

"What time is it?" I ask quietly.

"Early." His sleep-roughened voice sends skinny tendrils of arousal spreading through my body. Slipping my leg over his body, I slide myself up to straddle his hips.

"Too early?" I ask.

Lukas chuckles sleepily, running the backs of his fingers over my cheek. "For this? For you? Hell no." His dark hair is tousled, and when he grins, it gives him a wild, dangerous look.

He slides his hands under the hem of my t-shirt, sitting up to lift it over my head. His arm wraps around my back, pressing my body to his, while his free hand tunnels into my hair, holding me while his lips brush mine in teasing little caresses.

I try to deepen the kiss, but his grip in my hair tightens, refusing to give me an inch. The movement makes the muscles in his back flex under my fingers and I shiver, loving the way he uses his power over me. Opening my eyes, I find him watching me heatedly.

He leans in, brushing a kiss over my lips. "You want to be in charge?" he asks, biting my lip softly.

I shake my head a little, smiling when he growls his approval, pulling my hair back, and exposing my neck to his mouth. His cock hardens under me, making me squirm. I hate that we're separated by all this stupid underwear.

His hand cups one of my breasts, squeezing gently before his thumb rasps over my nipple. I gasp, pleasure spiraling through me, as I arch my back. Lukas dips his head, drawing the other nipple into his mouth, his tongue flicking over the tight, aching tip.

"Lukas!" I gasp when he bites me. It's gentle but firm enough to make me jump. The edge of pain melts away into pleasure almost instantly, and I can't help rocking against his lap. His steel length rubs the length of my slit, making me aware of just how slippery and wet I feel.

Lukas' hands leave my body, gripping the edge of my panties and ripping them in a swift show of force. He shoves them down the other leg before laying back. Winding his arms under my thighs, he drags me up his body. I yelp as my hands hit the padded headboard, steadying myself as my knees sink into the pillow on either side of his head.

"What are you doing?" I gasp.

Oh, sweet Lord. He is face-first in my business and I'm too stunned to think anything other than terrible dirty thoughts. Lukas gives me a devilish smirk, too pleased with himself to hide it.

"I'm getting my breakfast, what does it look like?"

"You can't— Like that? You'll suffocate!"

"Then I'll die happy," he says with a roguish wink. His arms wrap around my thighs, pulling me down on his face and I want to argue but—

"Oh my God." I moan instead. His tongue slicks up the length of my folds, teasing and exploring and swirling around my clit before doing it all over again. He sucks my bud between his lips, groaning and digging his fingers into my thighs.

"OhmyGod.OhmyGod.OhmyGod," I whisper, clinging to the headboard for dear life as he does something with his tongue that I don't think I can name or even properly describe. One of his arms shifts, pushing me forward as a finger sinks into my core. His other hand grabs my butt, grinding me against his face, and I gasp with pleasure.

"So good," I moan.

Lukas makes a growling sound as he watches me, his eyes intense. Tingling arousal spreads through my bloodstream, wrapping itself up my spine. Mewling little sighs keep working their way out of my throat, spurred on by Lukas' wicked tongue. I momentarily lose myself working my hips against his mouth, trying to get the angle just right, but I don't want to suffocate him, so I stop.

He lands a smack on my butt cheek, growling against my clit as he grips my hip again, rocking me against his face roughly. That's a clear, "don't stop" if I ever saw one. Honestly, he's so big, it's not like he couldn't overpower me if he wanted to...

Letting go of the last of my doubts, I close my eyes and give in. Fire curls in my belly, threatening to consume me, and when Lukas pushes another finger inside me, pressing and stroking, I let it.

I fall apart, a screaming, quivering mess as Lukas holds me down, his grip firm, refusing to let up until he's coaxed every last drop of pleasure from my body.

I come down, relaxed but exhilarated as he lets me slide sideways off him. I prop myself against the headboard, half-reclined next to his head as I try to get my brain straight. I'm naked except for the ruined panties dangling off my right ankle. A laugh bubbles out of my chest as I lift my leg to show him the damage.

"You've got to stop ripping my panties every time we fool around. I only have so many, you know."

Lukas unhooks the cotton remains from my foot, sitting up and throwing it across the room. He rolls to his hands and knees, climbing over me with predatory heat in his eyes.

"If you stop wearing panties, there's nothing to ruin. Or get in my way," he says, kissing his way up my body. His beard tickles my skin and I can smell the subtle scent of sex on him. I still can't quite believe I just did that to his face, but holy hell was it sexy. His cock is rigid between his thighs, flushed and tempting.

Reaching down, I wrap my hand around his stiff length, stroking him in my fist.

"I want you inside me," I say boldly. He's asked me to tell him what I want and speaking like this is... liberating, though still a little terrifying.

Lukas groans, biting my shoulder. "I'll give you anything you want, baby girl," he says before standing to retrieve a condom. He tears the packet open with his teeth, sheathing himself before kneeling at the end of the bed, eyeing me with a crooked smirk. Grabbing my ankles, he pulls me down the bed, rolling me onto my side in one swift motion. I laugh, but a little shiver runs through me at the show of strength. I *love* it when he manhandles me a bit.

He straddles my lower leg, hooking the top one over his shoulder, grabbing my hips, and pulling me closer. He growls again, running his thumb through the arousal slicking my entrance, and dragging it up to my clit. The thick head of his shaft stretches me as he leans forward, burying himself deep. I'm so full of him that it blocks out everything else. He's all I can think about and all I can feel.

"Fuck," he mutters, eyes rolling back in his head. I love watching him like that. That I can make him feel so good... it's powerful.

"You're so goddamn tight, baby," he says as he drags himself all the way out, impaling me again with more force and speed.

"Lukas!" I gasp, breathing hard with pleasure.

"Too much?" he asks, freezing in place, worry creasing his brow.

"No," I moan. "Don't stop! Give me more," I plead.

His eyes flare, a muscle ticking in his jaw as he pulls out, thrusting back in, deep and hard.

"Yes," I gasp.

"God, I love this greedy little pussy," Lukas mutters, surging into me and dragging back out. He turns his head, biting the inside of my knee. The little nip echoes through my body in waves of building pleasure that makes my pussy clench around him. Lukas grins, a devilish, self-satisfied smile as he moves his lips, biting me again and swearing under his breath when my body responds.

Still on a high from my last orgasm and being driven to another, I give myself over to his intoxicating rhythm. Lukas' body is practically humming with dominant energy, a little drop of sweat trails down his shoulder, following the line of his tattoo.

"You like that big cock, don't you," he growls, giving my ass a smack. Heat spreads through my core, throbbing and insistent.

"God yes," I moan. He ducks under my leg, crossing it to his other shoulder. My abdomen twists and the new angle has Lukas stroking my g-spot on every thrust.

"Such a good girl. Tell me what you want," he demands, his voice low and rough with need. My heart is thundering in my ears. I'm so close and overwhelmed, it's hard to focus on what he's saying.

"I want you to make me come," I whimper. "Oh God, please make me come."

"Who's my girl, Parker?" he asks, cracking a palm against my backside. It's more noise than pain, but he glides a hand over my butt cheek, rubbing the slight sting into tingling warmth.

"I am," I moan.

"Who makes you feel good, baby?" Lukas circles my clit with two fingers, licking the thumb of his other hand.

"You do!" I sob.

"Fuck yes, I do. God, you've got a pretty ass." He presses the pad of his thumb against my puckered entrance, rubbing with unrushed persistence and oh-my-freaking-God. That feels way better than it has any right to.

"Come for me, baby. I wanna feel that pretty pussy soak my dick," he growls. "Say my name and come on my dick. Who's got you, Parker?" The edge I've been teetering on disappears. I fall, screaming out his name, my body trembling. I feel him shudder his release, shaking with the effort of holding me and staying upright. He slips out and collapses next to me on the mattress.

"Fuck," Lukas gasps for air, an arm thrown over his eyes as one hand searches for me dramatically. I laugh, too blissed out to react when his hand wanders over my stomach and settles on my breast. "Is there a respectful way to imply you have a magic pussy?" he pants.

"You're a born romantic, you know that?" I tease with a grin. Thank you, endorphins, because I feel incredible right now. I'm so happy I could just float up into the clouds and bob around like a balloon on a string.

Lukas composes himself, at least as much as he can. He rolls over to face me, cupping my cheek and kissing me. It's soul-achingly sweet, and he draws it out until my heart is pounding.

"I'm glad you stayed. Thanks for not running off in the night."

"You're welcome," I giggle.

"You wanna go back to sleep?" he asks.

I shake my head. "I don't think I could. I slept like the dead last night. Besides, now I'm wide awake."

Lukas grins at me. "Shower?"

"Yes, please!"

We take our time in the shower, partly because Lukas insists that he should get to wash me and can't be hurried. I don't mind. And I take my time polishing his tattoos. His body is a work of art. Every time I look at his ink, there's more to appreciate and underneath it... whew. His broad powerful frame makes me feel delicate next to him and that's not something I'm used to. My dad always said I came from "solid Midwest working stock" just like him. I don't think he meant it to be hurtful, but no teenage girl likes being compared to cattle. I was always thicker than my wispy mother, and he never let me forget it.

It's hard to feel bad about myself right now. Not when a man as sexy as Lukas watches me like he can't get enough. I swear his hands never leave my body. He performs his entire morning routine with half his body. The other half is stroking my hip, running a hand over my back, or grabbing my butt. My favorite might be the way he tugs my hair a little each time he kisses me. It's just a playful little thing, but it stirs all kinds of filthy memories.

We drive over to the bakery for breakfast because Lukas seems to be as bad as I am about picking up groceries. He's also stubborn as hell about the truck. No matter how many times I tell him I should get a rental, he won't hear of it.

"I don't need it. I never drive it in the summer," he argues as I park in the lot down the road from my store. "Besides, I like watching you drive it. It's sexy as hell."

"I'm starting to think you feel that way about most of the things I do," I tease back.

He tugs one of my curls and leans in so I can feel his warm breath on my lips. "Then you're paying attention, Freckles." He smirks a little when I shiver.

Lukas wraps a hand around my waist as we walk into the bakery and I have to admit, I'm a little nervous about how Lilah will react. We left everything on a good note yesterday, but this is the first time I've been out in public with Lukas, our yelling match on the street yesterday excluded. Just thinking about that makes me wince.

He stands behind me while we wait in line, yanking my card out of my hand when I try to pay and handing the cashier his card instead.

"Thanks Ashley," he says, grinning at my scowl.

We wander over to the dining area and claim a small table before he heads back to pick up our food. I'm relieved when we make it all the way through our coffee and muffins and it's still just the two of us. The easy intimacy between us makes me feel like I've known him for years and as much as I love his sisters, I wouldn't give this feeling up for anyone.

"Are you busy Friday night?" Lukas asks over his cup of coffee.

"No... but I know you have your family dinner. I can meet you after or—"

"Or you can come with me," he interrupts.

"You don't have to—"

"Parker," he interrupts again, leaning forward with a sweet, crooked smile. "Eventually you're going to realize that I like being with you, and then you're going to feel really silly for trying to talk me out of this."

"Sorry," I laugh softly. I'm not used to feeling wanted like this. I have a lifetime of conditioning that's telling me to stay out of the way. "I would like to go with you."

His grin grows, lighting up his face. "Good."

"If we're going to be together that night, I feel like I should tell you Friday is my birthday," I tell him with a wince. "I don't want to make a big deal out of it. I just felt wrong not saying anything..."

"Seriously?" he asks, eyebrows scrunched. "What were you going to do if we weren't together?"

I shrug. "Not much. It's not a big deal."

Lukas' eyes narrow as he looks at me, his smile vanishing. "Shot in the dark here, but I'm guessing your parents weren't big birthday party types."

Not for the first time, a cold weight settles in my stomach at the thought of my birthday. Middle River wasn't exactly a hotbed of Pinterest-worthy kid's parties, but I know most of the kids got presents, pizza, and cake. My mom would sometimes cook a meal I liked on my birthday. Presents weren't a thing. I was told that we celebrated accomplishments, not the arbitrary day we were born.

I try to smile at Lukas while I shake my head but end up mostly just pressing my lips together. "It's fine. I don't want to make a big deal out of it."

"For the record, I don't think I like your parents," he says through tight lips.

I shrug and give him a little laugh. "That's ok. I don't like them either, and it's not like they'll be a part of my life anymore." That thought cheers me up considerably. I *never* have to go back and the odds of them bothering to look me up, let alone contact me, are precisely a snowball's chance in hell.

Lukas takes my hand in his, pressing my knuckles to his lips and holding them there as he looks at me for a long second. It's a gesture filled with so much sweet affection that it makes my breath hitch.

My heart pounds when he looks at me like that and I realize that it's not just chemistry or shallow lust. I'm in love with him. As crazy as it sounds, I feel it in every cell of my body. I'm in love with Lukas Donovan... and I'm in way over my head.

22

LUKAS

I have a little time before I'm due at the shop, so I walk Parker across the street, refusing to take the truck for about the tenth time this morning. I finally convince her to keep it by reminding her that this way she can run home for more clothes and check on that neighbor's dog she loves so much.

I kiss her goodbye and start the short walk to my auto shop. My thoughts are clanging around after our conversation. Part of me wants to destroy everything her parents have, just to punish them for the way they treated Parker. The rational side of me can at least acknowledge that she wouldn't be here if it wasn't for them. I'm not glad for the cause, but I can't say I'm sorry she had to get away and start over here.

From the bits and pieces I know or can guess at, her past is a flaming shitshow. It's almost hard to believe what an amazing person she is, considering her upbringing. I can't fix any of that crap, but I *can* give her a much better future. Starting with her birthday.

The more I think about it, the more excited I get. I'm not sure exactly what I'm going to do, but I've got a couple ideas. By the time I get to the shop, I've got a list going in my head and a group text pinging away on my phone. Unsurprisingly, my sisters are on board and taking over within seconds.

THE WEEK BLOWS BY, going down in history as the best week of my life. I wake up to Parker in my bed every morning; I visit her for lunch every day, and we go home together at night. No matter how much time we spend together, I can't get enough of her. It's insane, but I think I'm going to ask her to move in with me. I just don't know if I can convince her to do it. I know she likes the idea that she's out on her own, doing it all herself. She doesn't want to be coddled or controlled. I don't want to do either of those things; I just want to be with her at the end of every day, and she keeps saying that her place is too small to have me over.

I'm mulling it over Thursday morning when I'm interrupted by a delivery. Mixed in with the car parts is a small package from an office supply company with my name on it instead of the shop's. I feel the grin spread across my face. I've been so distracted that this completely slipped my mind.

Checking the clock, I note that it's a little early for lunch, but I can't wait to see Parker. Grabbing my stuff, I yell at Asher across the bay as I buckle my helmet.

"I'm going to lunch!"

He rolls his eyes and waves me off. Grumpy bastard needs to get laid. I rev the engine a couple times to annoy him before pulling out.

Parker is ringing up a customer when I walk into her shop, the package under my arm. I lean against the front window, waiting for her to finish. She's wearing a white tank top tucked into a swingy little red skirt that keeps giving me tantalizing views of her thighs. We slept in this morning, and she refused to be late opening the shop, even if it was because I wanted to eat her pussy. Maybe I'm a horny bastard, but I'm hurting for a fix. She grins at me from behind the counter as I look her up and down, giving her a lascivious smirk.

The little old lady glances at me, eyes widening as she adjusts her glasses. She doesn't take her eyes off me as she whispers to Parker: "There's a hoodlum in your store."

Parker laughs. "That's okay. He's my hoodlum," she says with a wink in my direction.

"Oh! Well," she replies, giving me another look, this one more approving than the last. "In that case, good for you."

Parker laughs again and hands the woman her change. "Thanks. Have a nice day."

I wink at the old broad as she leaves the store. She gives me one last look from head to toe with a muttered, "Oh my."

As soon as the door shuts and we're alone, Parker breaks out in peals of laughter. "Oh my," I repeat as I walk closer to my girl.

"You saw this outfit before we left this morning," she reminds me.

"I can't help myself when you wear little skirts like that though," I say, craning my head so I can get a better look at her legs behind the counter. She leans her elbows on the counter and pops a foot up behind her, her curvy ass giving me the dirtiest thoughts.

"I aim to please," she says. "What's in the package?"

"Early birthday present." I grin, setting it on the counter and ripping into it. Parker gives me an adorable, thoroughly confused face. I just wink at her and drag her decrepit typewriter towards me. Emptying my pockets, I pull out a clean rag, a small bottle of rubbing alcohol, and a pair of black nitrile gloves. She watches me pull the gloves on, biting her lip so I flex my arms and give the glove a little snap.

"Wanna play doctor?" I tease. Parker's eyes flare, a blush tinting her cheeks and I'm instantly hard. Of course, she does. "You are fantastically kinky, you know that Freckles."

"I'm— I am not!" She sputters. "Well. Ok. Maybe a little. I'm blaming the romance books, though."

Leaning over the counter to kiss her, I give one of her curls a little tug and nip her lip softly. "Then I should thank the books because I fucking love it," I tell her.

Parker leans on the counter, chin resting on her fist, watching in fascination as I take out the old, dried up ribbon, and clean the machine up with the alcohol and tiny wire brush. I test each key, carefully bending the arms back into place until each one moves freely and falls back into place with a satisfying clunk. Once I install the new ink ribbon, I slide the repaired typewriter back towards her.

"You have printer paper, right? Give it a test run."

She spins with a grin on her face, pulling the paper out of a cubby under the counter. She feeds a piece in and plunks away. When she hits the return key, the machine makes a satisfying ding that makes her smile harder every time. When she's done, she pulls the paper free and hands it to me.

Thank you! You're the best.
I can't believe you did this for me.
Also, you've got a great butt...

LAUGHING, I fold up the note and put it in my jeans pocket. "I'm keeping this."

"How in the world did you know how to do that?" she asks. The look on her face is pure affection and adoration, and it makes my chest swell. No one looks at me the way she does, and I fucking love it.

"Youtube," I shrug and run my hands through my hair. "Plus, you know, the whole mechanic thing. This is nothing compared with a car engine."

"True," she laughs with a smile. "Still... I feel like I should give you a reward or something..." her voice goes all soft and breathless, her eyes hooded as she rounds the counter, running a hand down my chest.

Every drop of blood in my body heads south when she uses that voice. God help me, she is so fucking sexy.

"Do I get to choose my prize?" I ask, smirking at the way she shivers.

"That only seems fair."

I rip the gloves off my hands, placing my hands on her hips and pushing her back around the counter. I know exactly what I want. With her back to the door, I press her backside into the counter, dropping to my knees in front of her. Her breath hitches, her eyes flaring with lust as I run my hands up her legs and under her skirt. I slide her panties down her legs, taking the black silky material and pocketing it.

There's a wooden stool next to me that Parker sits on when she's bored or reading. Lifting her foot, I set it on the stool, spreading her legs wide. Her skirt edges up her thigh, barely concealing her pussy. I push the red material up slowly, watching her face. One of my favorite things about Parker is the way she looks when she's turned on like this. The pink flush that spreads down her cheeks and chest, her shallow, panting breaths, and those blue eyes, open so wide like she doesn't want to miss a second of what I'm going to do to her.

Running two fingers over her glistening entrance, I'm not surprised to find her slick and wet, already excited for me. She's so goddamn responsive to my touch. She trembles when I push them inside her, moaning as I flex them, pulling out and stroking into her again. She furtively glances over her shoulder at the door.

"What if someone comes in?" she asks breathlessly.

"You better come quick so we don't find out," I grin up at her before flicking my tongue over her clit. She throws a hand over her mouth, muffling herself as she cries out. I don't draw it out. I zero in on exactly what she likes, starting gentle and ramping up, painfully aware that someone could walk in at any moment. I should have locked the damn door, but it's too late now.

Parker is shaking, whimpers slipping past her fingers as I suck her swollen clit between my lips and fuck her pussy with my fingers. She's so wet, her arousal coating my hand as I pump into her with punishing thrusts.

"Yes, yes, yesssssss," she moans, her body seizing up, pussy clenching and rippling around my fingers as the orgasm consumes her. She's so goddamn sexy when she comes. It makes me want to do it over and over just to watch. What I really want right now is to bury my cock in her and make her come on my dick, but I've already pushed my luck taking her like this. Slipping my fingers free of her, I lick them clean, loving the way she watches, lips parted.

Rising to my feet, I kiss her hard, stroking into her mouth with my tongue. "You taste incredible." I tell her as I tug her skirt back into place. She looks up at me, eyes burning as she rubs a hand over my aching hard-on. It's threatening to rip straight through my jeans and she's not helping. Gripping her chin, I turn her face up to mine.

"I'm keeping your panties. You can get them back tonight if you're a good girl," I tell her with a wink before stepping back and putting space between us.

She makes a sound halfway between a laugh and a groan. "Give them back. I can't walk around like this!"

I back around the counter, grabbing my stuff in a messy bundle before heading for the door. "Uh-uh. You said I could pick my prize." She rolls her eyes at me but lets me keep them.

"See you tonight, Freckles."

23

PARKER

It's nearly closing time when I get a text from Lukas.

Lukas: Hey Freckles. I've got a tow job. Going to be late. You've got my garage code, use it!

It's a nice thought, but I need to pick up some shop paperwork from my place and I'd like to check on Cujo and bring him a treat.

Me: Text me when you're done. I'm going to run home for a bit.

Lukas: I'd rather come home to you naked in my bed...

Me: You do still have my panties. Text me when you're *almost* done and maybe you'll get your wish...

Lukas: You're just torturing me now.

Me: I'd argue that I'm being a *very* good girl. If you disagree, you could always spank me later.

Lukas: Goddammit. How am I supposed to leave my desk when you write things like that? I can't think straight, let alone drive.

Me: Sorry! Go focus. Try not to think about my panties in your pocket.

All I get back in reply is a series of high-five hands, but I'm pretty sure those are meant to be promised spankings and a little shiver of excitement runs through me. It's going to kill me to wait for him.

Cujo is overjoyed to see me, gratefully takes the potato chips I saved him, crunching on the whole handful loudly. I scratch behind his ears and he stares into my soul as I tell him about my day, leaving out the dirty parts, obviously. He follows me along the fence line as I head to my bungalow, whining as I step inside.

"I'll bring you some peanut butter later," I promise. "I've gotta catch up on work." He just sits and cocks his head to the side. I don't think he caught anything besides "peanut butter."

I'm lying on my stomach in my loft bed an hour later, trying to decide which books to add to my inventory. I've read through so many book descriptions that my eyes are starting to cross when I hear shouting outside. This may not be the greatest neighborhood, but at least it's usually quiet. I can't resist a little drama though, so I close my laptop and climb down the narrow ladder.

When I crack my bungalow door, the shouting gets louder and I hear something whining. My heart clenches as I realize it's coming from right next door.

Cujo.

Flinging open the door and stepping outside I see my next-door neighbor standing over Cujo. The potbellied, sweat-stained man sounds drunk, slurring as he screams at a cowering, whimpering dog.

Physically I'm no match for that asshole and confronting him would be beyond stupid. I need help. Running to grab my phone, I tap through to Lukas' number as fast as I can, my hands shaking. He answers on the second ring. Thank god, he's good about keeping his phone nearby.

"Hey Freckles, I was just—"

"I need you here *now*," I interrupt.

"Address," he replies shortly.

I give him my landlord's address and tell him about the neighbor, relief washing over me as I hear his motorcycle rev in the background.

"I'm coming," he says. "I'm five minutes away, but I can't talk to you on the bike. Call the police," he says before hanging up.

I look at my phone, but my hands won't stop shaking. I'm trying to calm down and focus, but the yelling and whining are making my heart race. I'm no use in a situation like this. Too small and nonthreatening to be intimidating and too panicked to be levelheaded. All I can think about is Cujo and how scared he must be right now.

I'm dialing 9-1-1 when I hear a yelp from Cujo, and my mind goes blank. Before I'm really even aware of what I'm doing, I'm yanking open the chain-link gate to the neighbor's property, red clouding the edges of my vision.

"Don't you fucking touch him!" I scream. The rocky dirt is tearing at the bottom of my bare feet and it just makes me angrier. Poor Cujo, this is how he lives every day. Rocks and dirt and this shitty yard and this shitty man are all he has.

The man sways on his feet as he looks up at me. Surprise flashes in his little piggy eyes before he squints and starts shaking a finger at me. Cujo is curled up at his feet trying to escape, but the man has him cornered against the house.

"Get your fat ass off my property," he says with a sneer, but I don't stop. He smells like B.O. and stale beer, and there's sweat dripping down his bald head. The anger twisting his face really puts him over the top, though. He is without a doubt the most *disgusting* man I have ever laid eyes on. It's all I can do not to gag when I look at him.

"No!" I retort. "You get *your* fat ass away from Cujo!" I know I should keep my distance. I know it's stupid to get this close, but I will not let him hurt Cujo and if I have to put my body between them, I fucking will.

"He's my property," the man says through a curled lip. "And if he's going to chew my shit, I can punish him any way I damn well want." He stares me dead in the eyes and pulls his foot back to kick Cujo, and I snap.

I don't remember winding up, but the next thing I know, my fist is connecting with his squashy, reddened face. He reels back, shock and pain registering in those horrible beady little eyes. I might have enjoyed his expression, but a split second later, agony shoots through my hand and up my arm.

"Oh, Jesus!" I scream, cradling my injured hand to my chest. Oh my God. Who knew punching someone would hurt this bad?! "Ow! Mother trucker, ow, ow, OW!" My neighbor stares at me stupidly, too drunk or dumbfounded to react.

"Parker!" I hear Lukas yell my name just in time to see him come flying through the gate in dark jeans and his leather jacket. There's a murderous expression on his face as he stalks toward my neighbor and I wince as he throws his helmet back against the fence with all the force in his body. I know just enough about safety gear to know that helmet is a goner.

He storms towards me like an avenging angel and even through the pain, I have to admire his ability to simultaneously melt the panties right off my body while being absolutely terrifying.

He steps between me and Captain Potbelly, glowering down at him until the coward backs away. Only once he's sure the man isn't a threat does he look at me. He keeps his body angled to protect me, glancing back and forth between my neighbor, my hand, and my eyes. There's a muscle ticking in his jaw, betraying the rage he's suppressing.

"Show me your hand, Freckles." His voice is gentle, but there's a tightness around the edges of his mouth.

Cradling it carefully, I hold it out a couple of inches, whimpering in pain. My thumb looks wrong and bruising is already spreading from the oddly angled joint.

"Fuck," he mutters. "Well, that's broken."

"He was going to kick Cujo," I say defensively.

"Oh, I saw. I saw you clock him too," Lukas shakes his head and mutters. "Six to midnight over here," making me laugh despite the pain radiating from my hand.

Lukas sizes up the situation for a couple of seconds, flexing his fists, chest heaving with what I think must be the effort it's taking him to not hit Cujo's owner. The man eyes Lukas warily, swaying on his feet, but otherwise remaining in place.

Cujo takes advantage of the quiet moment to slink over to my side, leaning into my thigh heavily. I pet him with my good hand.

"Hey buddy," I say quietly, smiling at him as he licks my good hand.

Lukas claps his hands together, rubbing them and I can tell from the look in his eyes he's decided something. The drunk asshole jumps like someone took a shot at him. Not that he wouldn't deserve it. I

139

shouldn't take pleasure in the fact that he's scared shitless of my boyfriend, but I can't help myself.

"Right," Lukas says. "Parker, we need to get you to a hospital and we're taking Cujo with us." Despite the pain in my hand, I want to jump on Lukas and cover him in kisses right now. Of course, he wouldn't leave Cujo behind with this garbage person.

"You and that fat ass bitch can't take my fuckin' dog," the man argues, stepping towards Lukas. That was the single stupidest thing he could do right now.

Lukas grabs the man by his dirty white tank top, nearly lifting him off his feet. "Listen and listen good, you piece of shit," Lukas growls menacingly. I follow, reaching out to stop him from hitting anyone and getting charged with assault. My good hand lands on his bicep and I have an overwhelming sense of déjà vu.

He speaks slowly through clenched teeth, "Say one more word about my girl and so help me God, they will *never* find your body."

The drunk pushes at Lukas' hands ineffectively before giving in. "Fine. Take the stupid mutt. I'll get your ass thrown in jail," he hisses.

Lukas cocks his head to the side before releasing one of his fistfuls of dirty shirt. His arm whips back and for a split second, I'm sure he's going to hit him, but he doesn't. He yanks his cell phone out of his back pocket.

"You know, maybe you're right. Let's call the sheriff to come settle this. In fact, I've got Bobby right here in my contacts. He's a family friend, you know." The man's eyes are darting back and forth between Lukas' face and the phone, trying to keep up.

"Let's call him up." Lukas gets a head of steam, laying the sarcasm on thick as he continues. "I can tell him how I got here just in time to see you beating your dog and grabbing my girl, breaking her hand in the process. I bet they'd go real easy on you, assaulting a woman like that. And animal abusers get treated real nice in lock up. I bet you'd be real popular—"

"Just take the fucking dog," my neighbor interjects. "Never liked the piece of shit, anyway. Take him and get the fuck off my property."

Lukas gives the man a shove as he releases him, giving him a sarcastic salute before turning towards me, putting a hand on my lower back, and steering me towards the gate. Cujo is glued to my thigh as we head to the truck. Lukas opens the back door and pats the seat for Cujo to jump in, but the Rottweiler puts his front paws up on the floor well, scrambling awkwardly. I feel for him. That's exactly how I feel getting into the truck too.

Lukas sighs, scooping up the dog and lifting him into the backseat as though he weighs nothing. Cujo sticks his head out the window, a dopey smile on his face as Lukas closes the door.

He steers me gently towards my landlord's house. He's still shaking with anger and adrenaline, but he's doing an admirable job of keeping it together. "Get your things, I'm taking your sexy ass to the hospital so they can take care of that hand," he rumbles. I realize in a wave of guilt that he thinks I live in the main house.

"Oh," I say awkwardly, pointing at my bungalow. "I live there."

Lukas looks at me, confused, as he follows me to my front door. He squeezes in after me, peering around as I slip on a pair of shoes and grab my purse and phone. He takes my purse silently, locking the door behind us as we leave. His lips are pressed together so hard that they look pale.

"Why do you look pissed off?" I ask.

"We can talk about it later. I want to get your hand taken care of right now."

"I didn't break my ears or my mouth. We can talk now," I say stubbornly.

"Fine. I'm *pissed* that I'm just now learning that you've been living in a shed."

"It's a tiny home," I say indignantly. "It has running water and electricity."

"Fine," Lukas says through gritted teeth as we walk back towards his truck. "It's a shed, with running water, in the worst neighborhood I know of."

"It's not usually this bad," I argue, knowing full well he's right. It is a God-awful neighborhood.

"You're not coming back here," he says. "You're staying with me." There's a finality in his tone that makes me so angry I could spit.

"Excuse me? You don't get to dictate where I live!"

Lukas doesn't yell. He never yells. But his volume climbs as he runs his hands through his hair, looking exasperated. "Keep your panties on. I'm not dictating shit. You can live anywhere you damn well please. If you really don't want to live with me, you can move in with one of my sisters. Hell, I'll buy you any house you want! But if you think I'm letting the woman I love live in a shitty little shed next door to a dog beating psychopath, you're insane."

My feet stop moving. My heart races, pulse skittering through my body as the smile pulls at my lips. He pauses a few steps ahead of me, turning back with a sigh when he realizes I'm not walking anymore.

"Why are you grinning at me like that?" he asks loudly. "You were yelling at me five seconds ago and now you're just standing there smiling like *I'm* the crazy one for wanting you to be safe."

"You said you love me," I tell him, tipping my head and waiting for him to catch up with his own mouth.

"I did?" he asks, brows furrowed as he thinks for a second, trying to remember exactly what he said. "Well... I do. I fucking love you." He still looks exasperated, but a smile is threatening the edges of his scowl.

"You're mad because you love me," I say, smiling so hard it hurts.

"Yeah. I mean, I love you, but you make me fucking crazy. You know that, right? I get this panicked phone call from you with nothing but an address in a shitty area. So I race over here, showing up just in time to see you slugging that white trash and—Jesus, Parker. That was so stupid. You know that, right? What were you thinking?"

Lukas is shaking as he brushes his hair back with his fingertips. "You scare the shit out of me sometimes. I love you, but that was so stupid. He could have really hurt you, Freckles." His voice cracks as I step closer and stroke his cheek with my uninjured hand. I can see the fear and relief in his eyes. He looks less like a terrifying biker and more like a little boy, afraid for someone he cares about.

"I'm sorry I scared you," I whisper, sliding my hand behind his neck and pulling him down so I can brush my lips over his. "I love you too."

24

LUKAS

My heart is still jackhammering away in my chest as we head back to my truck. Elation from Parker's whispered "I love you too," is mixing with the sick worried feeling in my stomach over her hand, and the rage I'm still trying to suppress from dealing with that drunk neighbor.

I'd love nothing more than to stand here and tell Parker how much she means to me, but she's in pain and it's breaking my heart. That, and I don't trust that asshole next door to let this go. I need to get my girl out of here, for good, and take her to a hospital. The pain in her hand is only going to get worse as the adrenaline leaves her system.

Cujo is laying in the back seat but he peeks out when we get close, whimpering pathetically.

"Do you think he's hurt?" Parker asks, tears brimming in her eyes. "We need to take him to a vet. He needs X-rays," she says.

I stare at her, aghast.

"What?" she asks. "Why are you looking at me like that?"

"*You* need X-rays, Parker. *You* need to see a doctor," I tell her exasperatedly, gesturing to her broken hand.

I try to help her into the truck but she resists, pulling back. "No," she says, turning her chin up towards me, a mulish expression on her beautiful, tear-streaked face. "I'll go after we take Cujo to the vet."

"Parker, don't be stubborn. He jumped up into the truck—"

"You had to help him!" she reminds me. "He's whimpering. He's in pain and can't say anything! I can wait. We'll just get some ice to deal with the swelling."

"Okay," I say cajolingly, rubbing her back in an effort to coax her into the passenger seat.

"Promise?" she asks.

I grunt a reply that could go either way, but Parker is in too much pain to notice. I have NO intention of delaying her medical treatment, but I'll figure it out once we get out of here. She winces as I help her into the truck and buckle her seatbelt. The pain on her face makes my stomach roil. I can't stand it. I want to punch something and fix it for her all at the same time. I settle for dabbing at the tear tracks on her cheeks with the bottom of my shirt, tucking a flyaway curl behind her ear, and rubbing the freckle on her earlobe. She gives me a sweet smile filled with soft gratitude and affection as I close the door.

I round the hood of my truck, pulling my cell phone out of my pocket and clicking on Asher's name.

He answers as I'm climbing into the truck.

"What's up?" he grunts. I buckle my seatbelt, lock the doors and start the engine before getting into it with him. I'm half afraid Parker will jump out of the truck if it's standing still while she hears this.

"Parker broke her hand. I'm taking her to the hospital. We have this dog; I need you to pick him up and take him to the vet—"

Parker is already yelling at me as I try to explain the situation to Asher.

"No! He's scared! He needs me with him! You can't just pass him off to someone else—"

Asher is sighing in the background and I don't know how much he catches, but he gets enough. "She's intense, man. I'll meet you in the E.R. parking lot at Sonoma Valley Hospital."

"Thanks, man. Can you call Julia and ask her if she can meet us in the emergency room?"

Asher grunts and hangs up.

"—you promised me!"

"No, I grunted. And this is the best way to handle it, Parker. You can't walk around with a broken hand while we wait for a vet to see Cujo. He doesn't like that you're in pain any more than I do, and it's just going to stress him out more. Asher—"

She's weeping openly now, new tears streaming down her face as she pleads with me. "He doesn't know Asher, and he's going to be scared."

"Asher is a dog whisperer. Cujo will love him. Trust me. This is best for everyone. Asher can bring him back to my place when we get you home tonight. We'll spoil him rotten. I promise."

Parker clams up, swallowing hard and wiping tears away as she looks out the window and then back at Cujo. I'm driving carefully, but every bump in the road makes her wince and she can't hide how much it hurts. "Okay. Fine," she whispers.

Asher is already in the parking lot when we get to the hospital. We trade truck keys so he doesn't have to move Cujo. Parker opens the back door and gives the big dog a careful hug, pressing her face into his thick neck.

"Be a good boy, buddy. I'll see you later," I hear her tell him quietly. The big softy licks her face before I steer her towards the hospital doors.

"He'll be fine. Asher's got this; I promise." She leans into my touch as we walk inside but looks back at Cujo. I follow her gaze and see Cujo leaning up around the headrest and licking Asher's face. Yeah, they're going to get along fine.

The woman behind the desk at the ER gives me a disapproving look as she takes in Parker, cradling her hand, and I know what she's thinking. I know how I look; how this looks. Leather and tattoos do not an abuser make, but they sure help people jump to nasty conclusions.

I take the offered clipboard and help Parker fill it out. Her right hand is useless, and I doubt she'll be writing much of anything for a couple weeks.

145

"Insurance card?" I ask her.

She winces, not looking at me as she says, "I don't have insurance. Just put down that I'll pay out of pocket."

I nod and take the forms back to the desk, clipping my credit card under the metal clip. "Everything goes on this card," I tell the woman, ignoring the puckered expression she's giving me. "Everything."

I take my seat to Parker's left, putting my arm around her until a nurse comes to call us back. I was hoping we'd see my sister by now, even though I know she's in the pediatric wing. It's strange to think of her working with kids. Outside of the hospital, she's got a vocabulary that would make the rowdiest dock workers blush. How she keeps her mouth in check at work, I'll never understand.

The nurse eyes me and asks Parker if she wants to come back alone. Parker shakes her head and leans against my side. "No, I want Lukas with me." I can tell she doesn't get it. They're trying to get her alone to ask if I'm the one that hurt her, but she's too sweet and naïve to see it.

"Ok then," the nurse says with a tight smile. "Follow me." She leads us to a little room and pats a folded-up hospital gown on the bed. "You'll need to put this on. I can help you if you'd like?"

Parker scrunches an eyebrow and squints one eyebrow in confusion. "No, I'm fine. Lukas can help me." The nurse gives us another tight-lipped smile. "The doctor will be right in to check on you."

Parker yanks the privacy curtain shut and gives me an exasperated look as I help her take her shirt off. "Why on earth would I want her to help when I have my boyfriend right here? What a weirdo…" she mutters. I help her slip the hospital gown over her injured hand, careful not to jostle anything. I have to stop myself from shaking my head at her innocent confusion.

This is part of what I love about her. She doesn't understand why they would be worried about me. She doesn't see my tattoos, my long, wild hair, or motorcycle jacket and think of me as a danger. She sees me for who I am and loves me. And it's not despite those things either. She loves me for the tattoos and scruffy exterior, just as much as the soft squishy parts of me that I don't show most people. She loves me so much that she can't even begin to see me from their point of view.

Not for the first time, I feel like a lucky bastard that she took my hand and trusted me when I asked her to. Stealing her away to the beach was the best decision of my life.

I open my mouth to tell her all of this. To explain why the nurses are acting the way they are. To explain why they think I'm a threat, but I'm interrupted by a knock on the door frame.

"Miss Thompson? I'm Doctor Weaver. Can I come in?"

"Um… hang on. Tying this up real quick," she says, looking over her shoulder at me and mouthing, "That was fast." I nod and kiss the top of her head as I finish the last bow.

"All set," I say, pulling back the curtain. A short, stocky man cranes his neck up to look at me. He can't be more than five and a half feet tall. Still, I have to give him props. He doesn't back down when he notices how big I am.

I help Parker sit on the hospital bed, putting a pillow behind her back so she's more comfortable, and sit in the chair next to her. The doctor goes over a couple details before finally looking at her hand. He's careful as holds her wrist, getting a good look at the awkward joint and wincing at the swelling and bruising.

"How did this happen?" he asks her. Parker, unaware of how it looks, glances at me. I know the expression she's making is because she feels bad for worrying me.

"I punched someone," she tells him.

"I don't see any bruises on Mr. Donovan here," he jokes back drily.

"No. No! I didn't hit Lukas!" she says, alarmed. "My neighbor. I hit my neighbor. He kicked his dog. Well, my dog—" She's rambling, and it's not helping the optics here, but more than anything I'm worried about how much she's hurting. They haven't offered her so much as a baby aspirin yet.

"She's in pain. Can we please do something about that?" I ask the doctor.

His eyes tighten in my direction a little. "Obviously, we'll take some imaging and get a handle on the extent of the damage. In the meantime, we can get Miss Thompson on some pain medication."

The nurse from earlier reappears in the door with a clipboard.

"Mr. Donovan? I have a question about Miss Thompson's paperwork. Could you join me at the nurses' station for a minute?"

"Can't it wait?" Parker asks.

"I'm afraid not. This will only take a couple minutes, then he can pop right back," the nurse says with forced cheeriness.

Parker scrunches her eyebrows, glaring at the nurse. "Don't you have one of those wheelie carts? Bring the paperwork here."

I grin at the demanding tone of voice she's using. She's not forceful often, and I can't help but think how insanely sexy it is. The last thing I want to do is leave her alone right now, but I know they aren't going to let up until they're convinced I didn't hurt her.

"It's fine, Freckles. I'll be right back," I say, standing and kissing the top of her head, tucking her hair behind her ear before I follow the nurse out. The nurse takes me around to the far side of the nurses' station and starts repeating the paperwork I filled in when we arrived, question by question, slowly retyping my answers. We're only halfway through the first page when I hear Parker's voice rising from across the room.

"... would never lay a finger on me! ... Are you out of your damn mind? ... Excuse me?! No, I will not calm down!" I can hear the doctor trying to placate her, but clearly, she's not having any of it. "You think you can judge him because of how he looks? GET OUT!"

I round the desk in a second, heading for the room, half afraid she might punch the doctor and break her other hand. When I yank the door open, Parker is standing next to the hospital bed, her face fiery as she clutches her hand to her chest.

"I said get out!" she yells at the doctor. He's holding his hands up, trying to apologize, his eyes wide. I almost feel sorry for him. Whatever he said, it's obvious he didn't realize the hell he was about to unleash.

"Parker, it's ok. We'll get you another doctor," I try to soothe. "Come sit down,"

"This is bullshit," she mutters, calming considerably but refusing to sit.

Doctor Weaver takes this moment to try regaining control. "I'm very sorry, Miss Thompson. Why don't we get you that imaging and—"

"No," she replies icily. This controlled anger is somehow scarier than the yelling and it's hard not to grin at the wide-eyed expression on the doc's face. "I. Told. You. To. Get. Out. You're not my doctor anymore."

Doctor Weaver throws his hands up and walks out.

"Come sit down," I cajole. She lets me settle her on the bed again.

"Why are you so calm?" she asks, looking at me stone-faced.

"Because I knew. The second we walked in the door, I saw the looks." I smile and shrug, trying to convince her that it's not a big deal. "It's fine. It just comes with the territory," I say, gesturing to myself.

"It's not *fine!*" Parker says. Her face crumples and tears well up in her eyes. "It's bullshit! They don't even know you!" She turns her mouth towards the open door and yells, "THEY DON'T KNOW ANYTHING!"

I laugh and rub her back. "But you stood up for me, Parker."

"Of course, I did," she replies. Her brow wrinkles as if I'm out of my mind. She pats the bed, scooting over to make room for me on her good side. It takes some careful wiggling to get my big frame on the narrow bed without jostling her hand. Parker lays her head on my shoulder, her body pressed against my side and her injured hand resting on my chest.

"I'm not surprised you came to my defense. Not really. That's just you in a nutshell. You're basically a marshmallow until someone threatens something you love. You almost hulked out on that doctor," I laugh.

"Yeah, well... he would have deserved it, but I can only hulk out so many times in one day," she mutters, making me laugh. Parker lets me hold her in silence for a minute. I can feel her heart thumping against my side, hard at first but settling down with each passing minute.

"I'm grateful for you," I say, kissing the top of her head. "I'm not used to people standing up for me like that. For loving me fiercely."

"Your family loves you," she whispers.

"I know," I reply. "It's different though. You chose me."

149

Parker cranes her neck back to look at me, her eyes shining with adoration. "I did. And I'll keep choosing you." I cradle her cheek in my palm and kiss her, trying to show her how much that means to me.

A breathless Julia chooses that moment to fly around the corner in her purple hospital scrubs. "What did I miss?"

25

PARKER

Filling Julia in on my outburst has me steaming all over again. The only thing that keeps me moderately calm is the look on Lukas' face. The small smile would look smug to anyone else, but I know he's proud of me and grateful that I stood up for him. I hate that it's a novelty for someone to have his back, but I can't say that I feel any different. I've never had someone to lean on the way I leaned on Lukas today. It's been a shitty day, but here he is, holding me tight and stroking my hair.

The new doctor shows up a minute after Julia. The middle-aged woman with a sharp bob and severe features walks into the room like she owns it, but she has a friendly glint in her eye when she says, "Good evening, Miss Thompson. I'm Doctor Casler. I hear we've had some excitement this evening."

Lukas snorts behind his hand.

"Yeah, you could say that," I answer tersely. "For the record, my boyfriend is *not* abusive. I did this," I hold my hand up in front of me, wincing at the jolt of pain that runs through it, "punching a drunk douchebag who was kicking a dog."

The doctor raises her eyebrows at me.

"And I'm not sorry, either," I add.

"Very good," the doctor nods, looking down at the chart in her hands. "Let's get some imaging done and figure out our next steps. You're not one of our E.R. nurses," the angular woman says to Julia.

"No doctor, I'm his sister and her best friend. I'm not here in an official capacity," Julia says, unclipping her ID badge and slipping it into her pocket.

"Very good," the doctor says again. "I'll have someone bring you ice and something for the pain if you don't have any questions…"

I shake my head, happy to have her leave and get this show on the road. *Finally*. I'm given some ibuprofen and a bag of ice and whisked away for X-rays a few minutes later. When I get back, Julia jokes that my outburst is to thank for the speedy care.

"He had it coming," I grump at her as Lukas settles back in next to me, stroking my hair. My hand is throbbing angrily, despite the ice pack and medication. Part of me wishes they'd given me something stronger than Advil, but I guess I'm coping. I'm still salty about the way Lukas was treated and the longer I lay here, tired and in excruciating pain, the grumpier I get.

Julia laughs softly, grabbing me another blanket and spreading it out over my legs.

"No arguments here, sister. Between the three of us, I can't stand Weaver. He's a condescending prick, and I'm glad you yelled at him. Casler has a good reputation, though. The nurses all like her because she doesn't fuck around."

Julia dims the lights and sits in the chair next to my bed, digging her phone out of a pocket. The dim lights, the warmth of Lukas' body, and the repetitive stroking of his fingers through my hair lull me into something almost resembling a relaxed state. If it wasn't for the pain in my hand and the bustle of the hospital outside my room, I think I'd happily take a nap.

It's not long before Dr. Casler bustles back into the room. "The good news is you didn't break anything," she says without preamble. "Unfortunately, your thumb is dislocated. I'm going to give you a local anesthetic and we'll pop it back into place. You'll need to wear a stabilizing sprint and a sling for a couple of weeks, but it'll be good as new after that."

Lukas lets out a relieved breath, ruffling my hair. "And then she can go home?"

Dr. Casler cocks an eyebrow at him as she says, "Unless she'd like to terrorize a couple more of my colleagues, yes, she can go home after that."

Julia snorts next to me.

I'm a ninny so I turn my head, looking away as the doctor numbs my hand and relocates my injured thumb. I can't feel a thing, but once it's over, I look up at Lukas and he seems a little green around the gills. "Maybe you shouldn't have watched either," I tease.

Julia walks us to the doors before clipping her badge back to her top.

"Thank you," I tell her. "For sitting with us and for taking care of me."

Julia grins at me. "Anytime. Although, I'd really like to see you hit the next guy in person. It's not the same having it retold."

"Deal."

"You want me to have Olive drop off some food for you?" she asks.

"Oh my god, yes, please. I'm starving," I reply.

"I'll text her right now," she says as she leans in, giving me a careful kiss on the cheek before hugging Lukas goodbye. "I'll see you two at dinner tomorrow," she says with a wink.

It's dark when we finally exit the hospital. The summer heat warms my skin, and for once, I can enjoy the warmth instead of feeling smothered by it. After being stuck in that icebox of a building, it feels perfect. Lukas hovers over every movement I make, his hand on my back as we cross the parking lot to his brother's truck.

To my delight, Lukas' truck is back, parked next to Asher's. The windows are all rolled down and Cujo's wide face is hanging out the back window, tongue lolling happily. He whines when he sees me, prancing his paws in place like he can't contain his excitement.

Asher hops out of the truck and tosses Lukas the keys. "He drooled all over your backseat. Good luck with that," he says with a surly scowl. Lukas shrugs, returning Asher's truck key to him.

"Is he ok? What did the vet say?" I ask as Lukas opens the back door for me to greet Cujo. He sniffs my injured hand, investigating the sling and licking my fingers gently. "You're such a good dog," I tell him, scratching under his chin.

"Just bruises. Nothing serious," Asher grunts.

"Are you sure?" I ask.

"One hundred percent," he answers. "They did a full check-up, even took x-rays. He's an attention whore, that's about the only thing wrong with him. Damn near mauled the vet tech with kisses when she brought out the treats. He's got medication in the glove box. I didn't trust him not to eat it—"

"Medication for what?" I interrupt. "I thought you said he was fine."

"He is. It's just preventative stuff. Flea and tick, heartworm and shit. Oh, and he's up to date on vaccines now. And they brushed his teeth."

My lower lip starts trembling as I look at Asher. He took such good care of Cujo, and I'm so grateful. It was tearing me up not to be able to take him to the vet myself, and he really came through for us. He might be a grumpy ass most of the time, but he's a softy underneath.

"Ah shit," he mutters. "Don't you cry."

Lukas laughs and steers me towards the passenger door. "Don't swear at her. She's had a long day," he says over his shoulder.

"Yeah, a long day of assaulting men and dognapping. I can see how that would really take it out of a person," Asher mutters.

"Allegedly. I *allegedly* assaulted a man and stole his dog," I say as Lukas helps me into the truck, chuckling as he buckles my seatbelt.

Asher's lips twitch. "Sure. That'll hold up in court. You two have a good night," he says as he climbs into his truck.

"Thank you!" I yell out the open window. Asher gives us a wave as he backs out and drives away. Lukas leans on my open window, grinning at me. "What?" I ask. "You look awfully smug."

He raises his eyebrows and grins at me.

"Yes," I sigh. "Fine. You were right. I'm glad you asked Asher to take Cujo to the vet." Lukas leans in, kissing me deeply.

"You always know exactly what to say to turn me on," he teases.

"Oh, yeah?" I ask, raising my eyebrows at him. "My hand feels pretty good right now, you know."

"Ha! Nice try, temptress. It only feels good because you're still numb. If you think I'm going to do anything other than feed you and put your sexy ass to bed tonight, you are sorely mistaken."

I sit back in my seat with an exaggerated huff. "Fine, be withholding then."

Lukas chuckles and walks around the front of the truck to the driver's side, shaking his head and muttering something under his breath. A happy shiver runs through me. I love him. And he loves me. It seems so simple.

As it turns out, the numbing effect starts wearing off before we even get back to Lukas' house, and as much as I hate admitting defeat, dinner and bed sounds like an amazing plan right now. Olive is on the front porch with bags of food in her hands when we pull in.

"What on earth were you thinking?" she hollers at me as Lukas helps me out of the truck. "Julia said you punched a guy and then terrorized the hospital staff— Good lord that's a big dog!"

Cujo jumps out of the truck, wiggling with excitement before rolling in the grass. He looks so damn happy. And to think that I was worried about how he'd adjust.

"That's Cujo," I tell her. When I say his name, he jumps up and barrels towards me, ears flopping. Lukas steps in to keep him from jumping on me, but it's unnecessary. Cujo skids to a halt a foot away from me and leans his big bulk against my thigh, smiling up at me with pure love and adoration. "Good boy, Cujo," I baby talk, scratching him behind the ears with my good hand.

"So the dog abduction wasn't an exaggeration, then?" Olive asks.

Lukas shakes his head, giving Olive a look.

"And that's not going to blow back on either of you?"

"Nope," Lukas and I say in unison. He gives me a crooked smile that melts my insides. Stupid hand! The rest of me is in desperate need of some attention, but until the pain settles down, I'm afraid I'll be left unsatisfied.

"Jesus. You two are a pair. I can't wait to hear the whole story, but I guess I'll let you have until tomorrow." Olive blows us a kiss as she heads to her car. "You better strap in for some babying. Gran is going to lose it when she spots that sling." She tips an imaginary hat in our direction. "Have a good night, Bonnie. Clyde."

We don't have dog food for Cujo, but Olive included a takeout out container labeled: "Doggie dinner." When I open it, I burst into tears. Inside is a mountain of scrambled eggs, with shredded chicken and brown rice mixed in. She even topped it with crumbled bacon.

"Why are you crying?" Lukas asks, alarmed.

"They're all so nice! Your family— They're all so thoughtful and they keep doing more than I could ever expect or hope and then I feel bad for being surprised because of course they're amazing—"

Lukas laughs, catching my chin in his hand and kissing me tenderly.

"They're going above and beyond because they adore you. You inspire kindness because that's what you put out into the world." He wipes the tears from my cheeks, pressing kisses to my skin in their place. "It's one of the things I love most about you."

"Sorry, I'm just emotional. This day has been crazy," I say.

"It's ok. Tomorrow will be better," he promises, wrapping an arm around my shoulders and holding me carefully. He presses a kiss to the top of my head. "Come on. Dinner. Bed. Sleep."

As long as I'm with him, that all sounds perfect.

26

LUKAS

Parker grudgingly lets me help her get ready for bed. It was bad enough watching her struggle to eat dinner with her left hand, but I drew the line when she started fighting with her shirt.

"Just let me help you!" I say exasperatedly.

"No," she argues. "You can't undress me, it will just turn me on and then I can't do anything about it."

I sigh, sliding a hand under the hem of her shirt. She makes me crazy sometimes. "I promise it won't be sexy. I'll make a stupid face the whole time."

"It won't help," she mutters, acquiescing to my touch. I help her get her good hand out of the shirt and lift it over her head before easing it down her injured arm. I do my best to be a gentleman but the sight of her standing there in that lacy bra and red skirt, knowing I can't fuck her is straight torture.

"That's not a stupid face," Parker grumps up at me. "Those are "fuck-me-dirty-bedroom-eyes.""

I bite my lip, holding back a smirk as I help her out of her bra and into one of my clean t-shirts. She shimmies out of her skirt and tosses it into her duffle bag with the rest of her dirty laundry. She climbs into bed, sitting propped up against the headboard, watching as I find a comfy blanket for Cujo to sleep on.

The big goof licks my face gratefully when I bend down to lay it out for him next to Parker's side of the bed. He spins in circles on top of it before I can get it smoothed out, thunking down on it happily, which makes Parker laugh.

"I guess that'll do then," I say, scratching his head.

"Thank you," Parker says. "For taking us in like this." She's still smiling, but it's tight around the edges and I know what she's thinking. I know the lasting damage and self-doubt a parent can inflict when it's clear they don't want you.

"I want you here, Parker. I was going to ask you to move in, anyway. This was just the best excuse to speed up the process. I meant what I said, you can live anywhere you want... but I want you here and I'll fight to keep you."

Reaching back, I grab my shirt and pull it over my head. Parker moans and flops sideways on the bed.

"Well, if you keep doing that you're going to have to fight to keep me off of you!" Her voice is muffled by the pillow she's buried her face in.

"So, I should find sweatpants to sleep in?" I tease her.

"Yeah," she sits up with a grin. "Or maybe like a velour jogging suit? That might dampen the sexiness..."

I pretend to gag. "I can promise you there's not a single item of velour anything in my closet."

Parker laughs. "Now I know what to get you for Christmas."

I snatch a pair of sweats from a drawer, drop my pants, and put on the sweats, trying to ignore the way she watches and licks her lips.

"Stop it, Freckles!" I shake a warning finger at her. "You're not going to tempt me!"

"But it's my birthday," she says with an exaggerated pout.

"No, it's your birthday tomorrow," I argue.

"Fine... I guess I can wait," she sighs.

I get in bed next to Parker, slipping an arm under her so she can lay her head on my shoulder. She rests her splinted hand on my chest gently.

"I love you, Parker," I say, kissing the top of her head.

"I love you too, Lukas," she sighs, her breath tickling my chest.

She drifts off quickly, and I lay awake for a long time, listening to her breathe. She scared the ever-loving shit out of me today. I don't know how I'm going to let her out of my sight ever again.

27

PARKER

I wake up to the sun shining through the curtains. The spot next to me is empty, but just as I sit up to look for Lukas, I hear the door shut downstairs and the scrabble of Cujo's paws as he tears upstairs. The big goof jumps his front paws on the edge of the bed to greet me, wiggling with joy.

Lukas follows, less wiggly, more devastatingly handsome, a bag of food from Olive's in one hand, a travel tray with two coffees in the other. I sit on the edge of the bed, bare legs hanging out from under my t-shirt as I pet Cujo. I don't miss the hungry way Lukas eyes me before he shuts it down, putting on a friendly smile.

"Hey birthday girl," he grins at me, setting everything down on the side table. "I was going to make you breakfast in bed, but I'm a terrible cook. This seemed like the kinder option."

He leans in, holding my neck and kissing me deeply. The scruff of his beard tickles my face as he draws my lip between his teeth, giving me a playful bite. I hold back a moan, desire creeping through my sleepy body.

"How's the hand?" he asks as he opens the bag.

"Surprisingly good, actually," I say, inspecting my thumb under the edge of the splint. The bruising looks horrible, but it really doesn't hurt as long as I don't move it.

"That's great." He grins as he pulls a stack of containers out of the bag. "Pancakes or waffles?"

"I can have whatever I want?" I ask, ignoring the containers of food and eyeing his belt. He doesn't catch it though. He's too busy sorting out the food and seems determined to keep this as PG as possible.

"Of course, it's your birthday," he says as he glances over at me.

"Good," I say as I reach for his belt with my left hand. "Because I want you."

Lukas bites his lip, closing his eyes and taking a deep breath before stilling my hand. "You're hurt. I don't want to make it worse."

"You won't," I laugh. "I'll keep my hand out of the way. I'm pretty sure I can do plenty with lefty." Sliding my palm over the bulge in his pants, I run my fingers over the outline of his hard-on. It twitches against my touch and I feel a little rush of self-satisfaction. "See."

Lukas' head drops backwards, eyes closed as he takes a shallow breath. His broad shoulders look tight as he wrestles with the desire to give in. He makes me feel like a vixen, but I kind of love it.

"Parker—" he chokes out one last protest, but when I unzip his pants and slip my hands into his boxers, he grabs my wrist. "Ok, you win, Freckles," he growls. "But there are going to be rules. And if you break the rules, I *will* stop. Got it?"

I smirk up at him, loving the way his eyes go dark with lust when I say, "Yes sir."

Lukas slides his hands up my thighs before spreading them wide and stepping between them. His eyes burn into mine as he lifts my shirt over my head, easing it over my splinted hand.

"What are the rules?" I ask coyly as he tosses it aside.

Lukas leans down, wrapping my hair around his fist, pulling it so I have to look straight up at him. Maybe it's messed up, but holy hell does it turn me on. His other hand cups my breast, rolling my nipple between his thumb and forefinger, giving it a little squeeze that makes me gasp, pleasure coursing through my body.

161

"You're going to lie down and you're going to put your hand up on the pillow. If you move your hand, we're done until you get a doctor's note. The rest of your recovery will be so G-rated it would bore a Disney character."

"Fine," I laugh. "Is that it?"

"No. I get to blindfold you and make you come as many times as I want."

My sex clenches at the possessive edge in his voice, the intensity in his eyes as he watches me. I feel drunk when he looks at me like that. Like he would do terrible things to have me and *only me*. Moisture slicks my folds as I squirm and nod excitedly.

"Yeah, I'm not going to fight you on that one," I whisper, so turned on that I'm trembling.

Lukas steps away, grabbing a black bandana out of a drawer, folding it over, and rolling it to make an improvised blindfold. I tip my chin up, closing my eyes so he can tie it for me. He's careful not to pull my hair but pulls it snug enough that no light sneaks through. Then he scoops me up, thick arms flexing under me as he sets me in the middle of the bed. He puts a pillow under my hand with a growly reminder not to move it. The threat of an entirely sex-less recovery is enough to glue my arm to this pillow for as long as he wants.

"You are so fucking sexy," he rumbles, running his fingertips over my stomach. His weight shifts over me as his mouth closes around my nipple, hot and wet. He sucks and flicks at it with his tongue, sending little waves of pleasure spinning through my body. He pinches my other nipple in his fingers, rolling and plucking at it until it's tight and straining for more. He switches sides, cool air making my damp nipple pebble instantly. When his tongue swirls around the other, I gasp, arching my back and rubbing my thighs together, trying to ease the aching need that's building. The movement only makes it worse when I realize how wet I am. I feel a tug on my nipple as Lukas turns his head. Yeah… he didn't miss that. He chuckles softly, the sound vibrating through my nerves.

"Spread your legs, Parker," he demands. I shiver and I do what he says, spreading my legs. "Wider," he growls, biting the underside of my breast, just hard enough to make me suck in a breath. I gasp, moaning as I spread my legs wide. "Good girl." His breath tickles my skin as he lowers his head, trailing little bites down my side. Goosebumps cover my skin and I feel electric, every inch of me tingling.

"Jesus, you're drenched," he growls, running a finger through my folds. I moan, the touch is so slight that all it does is make me needier. His finger pulls away and then I feel the damp pad of his finger pluck at my nipple. He sucks the tight peak into his mouth as I feel his fingers at my entrance. He pushes them inside, groaning into my breast.

"Holy shit," I pant, my head spinning at the rush of erotic satisfaction. "Oh God, yes," I whisper as his fingers twist inside me, solid and thick. He drives me higher with each stroke until I'm shaking. The mattress dips beside me as he moves lower, and when I feel his tongue flick against my clit, I come, moaning his name.

I run my good hand through his hair as I float back into my body. His bristly cheek rests on my thigh, his fingers moving in me slow and gentle.

"Mmm..." I sigh. "That was amazing."

"That was one," he growls.

I laugh, stroking his hair again. "How many times are you planning to do that?"

"At least two more." He bites my inner thigh before licking my pussy from opening to clit with a broad flat tongue.

"Oh!" I cry out, digging my fingers into his scalp. Blindfold or not, my eyes roll back in my head as he tongues me, pulling my already sensitive clit between his lips. My orgasm tears me apart in seconds, so fast that it could have been part of the first one, but Lukas draws out the third, bringing me to the brink and backing off until I'm begging to come.

"Not yet," he mutters. "I want to feel you come around me. Ask me for this dick. Beg me to fuck you and I'll let you come."

I feel feverish. I'm all exposed nerve endings desperate for relief. "Please. Please fuck me. Please let me come on your cock," I whimper. I hear the ripping of a foil packet and the telltale sound of a condom being rolled on.

"Watch that hand, baby." I don't know how he knew, but I was about to reach for him, carelessly, with my injured hand.

He chuckles softly, kneeling between my legs. His hand slides under my tailbone, fingers pressing into my back as he lifts my hips. The fat head of his erection strokes against my slippery folds before tapping on my swollen clit, sending stars dancing behind my eyelids.

"Please-please-please," I moan into the dark.

"I can't deny you anything," he says as he thrusts deep. I'm so wet, so turned on, my nerves so raw; being filled like that in one heavy stroke is overpowering. I gasp, grabbing his forearm with my good hand. It's all I can do to keep the injured one on the pillow as he pulls out slowly, every ridge and vein making my heart beat faster.

"Say you're mine," he says in a quiet, rough voice. I feel his fingertips run over my skin, trailing over my stomach, my breasts, and up the side of my throat. I can almost picture the intense, aching expression on his face as his eyes follow his fingers.

"I'm yours," I promise.

I feel Lukas lean over me as he sinks deep again, his chest scraping against my pebbled nipples as he claims my mouth.

"Fuck this," he mutters, pushing the blindfold up my face. "Say it again."

I blink at the morning sunshine, my heart humming. "I'm yours," I whisper. His tousled hair falls in his eyes and he shoves it back, pressing his forehead to mine, gaze penetrating, as he thrusts into me. Lukas palms the side of my neck, his fingers tangling in the hair at the base. He rubs his thumb over my lips, groaning when I lick the tip. He presses it farther into my mouth and I swirl my tongue around it, biting him gently. He moans and fucks me harder.

"Parker," he growls. He's close and I know he's trying to wait. He always puts me first. I pull his hand down to my throat, showing him what I want. Tentatively, I shift my hand down, rubbing my clit once. A pleased sound rumbles out of Lukas' chest.

"Jesus Christ, you're sexy," he groans. "Keep going. Rub your clit for me." He watches, mouth slack as I move my fingers in little circles. The rough pads of his fingers press the sides of my throat with careful pressure and a shudder of wicked pleasure tightens my core, heat blossoming and spreading.

"Oh-fuck-oh-fuck-oh-fuck-so-tight-oh-fuuu…" Lukas mutters, his eyes rolling back in his head. "Parker— fuck."

Watching him lose control, body shuddering, muscles clenching, pushes me over the edge. I come hard, body arching under his.

Lukas shifts to the side, lying next to me on the bed.

"Good God, woman," he pants.

"Magic pussy?" I laugh. He groans in good-natured agreement. "Best birthday ever," I say, rolling over to kiss him, groaning when I see the clock. For the first time since opening the bookshop, I'm tempted to take a day off. "Can we just lay in bed all day?"

"Freckles, I told you, I can't deny you anything."

28

LUKAS

I genuinely contemplate staying in bed with Parker until someone sends a search party, but eventually, she decides we should get up and go to work. I don't want her to take the splint off and she agrees to let me help her shower. I tie a plastic bag over her hand, and she has to hold it up out of the spray of the shower while I shampoo her hair. Somehow, I keep my hands from wandering too much, but I honestly couldn't tell you how.

Helping Parker get dressed is a whole other adventure. I've never put a bra on someone, and it is significantly more complicated than taking one off. Fumbling with the little hooks, I accidentally lose one side and end up swearing as I wrestle it back into place. She laughs uncontrollably at my grumping, but I enjoy the hell out of situating her tits in the cups. She finally pushes me back a step when I start playing with her nipples.

"Those are fine the way they are," she tells me with a grin. "Believe it or not, I'd rather not have the high beams on all day." She manages to slip her dress on without my help before stepping into her panties and pulling them up with just the one hand. I could have helped with that part if she'd asked, but I don't mind watching either.

"Am I going to get to keep these today?" she asks with an arched eyebrow.

"We'll see." I sweep my gaze up and down her body, leaning in to kiss her neck and giving her a little bite at the junction of her neck and shoulder. Parker shivers, a little moan stuck in her throat.

I reheat our breakfast and we eat while Cujo watches forlornly from next to his bowl of dog food. Clearly, he prefers my sister's takeout version of mealtime to dry food.

"You think he'll be ok here today?" Parker asks, looking at the enormous dog.

"Yeah, I'll come back and check on him and we can take him to dinner tonight. Gran won't mind."

Parker grins at me, her coppery hair drying into soft waves. "I almost forgot about dinner. What are you doing at the shop today?"

I clear my throat. I thought about this for ages last night after she fell asleep. "I thought I'd let Asher cover the shop, and I'd go get the rest of your stuff from your... tiny house. I don't want you going back over there unless you really need to. Besides, I need to get my bike. I kind of abandoned it."

She stops chewing her mouth full of pancakes and stares at me for a beat before swallowing roughly. "Are you *sure* you want me to move in—?"

"Positive," I interrupt. "But I'll keep telling you until you believe me. I want you to live with me. Besides, what would we do with our ill-gotten gains?" I ask, gesturing at Cujo. "I don't want to split custody," I say, winking at her. "So you'll just have to stay here with us and put up with endless orgasms."

Parker blushes, the color spreading to her hairline. "Well, I can't argue with that."

"And that's why I love you," I say, kissing her before standing to collect our plates. I add some leftover eggs and bacon to Cujo's dish. He wolfs them down, giving me big, grateful eyes. "I am going to spoil the shit out of you," I tell him before I catch Parker staring at me through half-hooded eyes, a soft smile on her face. "What?" I ask innocently.

167

She shakes her head, looking down. "Nothing. You're just a big softy and that's why I love you."

I drop Parker off at work, making sure she gets inside okay before calling my brother. He's grumpy about it but agrees to help me shuttle my bike back from Parker's rental before opening the shop on his own.

He's in a huff when I pick him up in front of his house. "This is insane. You know that, right? You can't fall in love with someone in less than two weeks. And asking her to move in with you? It's not rational."

I shrug at him, unbothered. "Say what you want, man. But I'm crazy about her. This is the right thing."

"How the fuck can you be so sure?"

I shrug again. "I can't explain it. I just know."

Asher scoffs and spends the next five minutes talking about the business. When we get to Parker's place, he takes my spare helmet and gets on the bike, shaking his head at me.

"Insane," he mutters.

I grab the key that Parker gave me and the stack of boxes I stashed in the back of the truck, tucking them under my arm as I head to her shed. Just looking at the damn thing pisses me off. Nobody notices me or says anything as I unlock the front door and go inside. I strip her bedding and toss it in a box with a small bag of laundry. I empty all the little cabinets and by "empty" I mean I pack up half a bag of coffee, a couple slices of bread, some peanut butter, and a single can of soup. Her little fridge has half and half. That's it.

Once I find all the odds and ends and pack them up, I'm left staring at two small boxes sitting on the floor. I'm shaking mad. I'm mad at myself for not noticing this before now, but she has *nothing*. These boxes, and the clothes at my house, are all Parker has in the damn world, and most of this is just bedding.

I'm all for keeping life simple, but the clothes and bedding are cheap and scratchy. Her laptop is a beat-up piece of shit and all of her food is some weird off-brand that I've never even heard of. She's done what she has to in order to get by, but in the process, she hasn't been able to treat herself to a single quality thing.

With a sigh, I double-check to make sure I didn't miss anything.

Spoiler alert, I didn't. Carrying her boxes to my truck, I catch her douchebag neighbor looking at me out a window. I jerk my chin at him and keep walking. He ducks away. Part of me wishes he'd come out looking for a fight. I'm in the mood to fuck something up and his face would do just fine. Not that Parker didn't do some damage already. I didn't miss his black eye and swollen cheek.

I make a couple of phone calls on the way home, hitting up my sisters for more favors. If it was for anyone else, I probably wouldn't bother, but I want things to be perfect for Parker. Not just today. Not just for her birthday. I want to give her everything she could want. Anything that would make her happy.

Cujo greets me at the door, winding his massive bulk around my legs like the world's largest, drooliest cat. He's so strong he nearly knocks me over. The big brute might look intimidating, but he's practically overflowing with affection. It's easy to see why Parker fell in love with him; I certainly don't mind having him around. He follows me around as I unpack Parker's boxes. It takes all of ten minutes.

"Come on, bud," I say to him, opening the front door. I grab the cheap little leash the vet gave Asher yesterday and head to the truck. He jumps up in the backseat on his own and rides with his head out the window all the way to the pet store. I let him sniff up and down the aisles, grabbing the bag of food he seems most interested in and every toy he picks up. He gets a new, black leather collar and a matching leash. The last stop is the engraver for his tags.

We finish up just before noon, so I take him by the bookshop to show off his new duds. Parker squeals with glee when I open the door and step inside with Cujo.

"Watch this," I tell her. "Cujo sit." He sits by my foot, looking up adoringly. "High five," I say, holding out my hand. He smacks a paw on it. I give him a scratch and plenty of praise as Parker walks toward us. He sits in place even though his front paws dance around, the desperation to see her leaking out of him. I can't blame him.

"Such a good boy, Cujo!" she says, bending down to kiss his big head and pet him with her good hand.

"Release," I tell him. His butt wiggles as he circles Parker, licking as much of her as he can get at. I can't blame him for that either.

Although, I make a mental note to get her in the shower before I lick her calves.

"You got him a collar!" she exclaims, blue eyes sparkling at me as she holds the tag in her fingers. I finger the spare in my pocket.

"Yeah, I didn't want him to get lost." Parker pats Cujo on the head and he wanders off to sniff the store. "My turn?" I ask, crossing the distance to her.

"Are you going to lick me too?" she teases.

"Absolutely," I say, burying my hand in her hair and pressing my lips to hers. She parts her lips eagerly, her tongue brushing mine. She tastes sweet, and I love the little moan she makes when I stroke her hip with my thumb.

We're interrupted by the chime of the bell over the front door. Two middle-aged women walk in, heading straight for the shelves of books. Kissing Parker on the cheek, I whisper, "Later," in her ear. She rewards me with a grin and a blush.

"I left your key under the landlord's back mat, like you said," I tell her, returning to a normal volume. "You're officially moved out."

"It wasn't a pain?" she asks.

I snort and try to cover it by clearing my throat, but the glare she gives me is enough to know I didn't succeed. "Sorry," I reply. "It's just you have no stuff. It took like twenty minutes. And even if it took all day, I wouldn't have minded. How does your hand feel?" I ask, changing the subject.

"A little achy and stiff but not bad, all things considered," she says, inspecting the hand hanging in the blue sling.

"That's great." I grin at her as we catch the two shoppers watching us out of the corner of their eyes and whispering. "I'll get out of your hair, but I'll pick you up at six for dinner?"

She nods happily. "Perfect."

I tip her chin up and kiss her, drawing it out before telling her, "I love you."

My heart beats faster when she says, "I love you too." I'll never get tired of hearing her say that.

"Come, Cujo," I say.

He peers around the backside of the counter at me, unwilling to leave Parker's space.

"Come on, bud! Let's go."

Parker laughs as he trudges toward me. I hate to drag him away when he so clearly doesn't want to go, but we have things to do.

29

PARKER

Despite the parade of customers that come through my shop, I feel like the rest of my day drags by. I don't see Lilah, Olive, or Julia all day and it sucks. I wish I had told them it was my birthday, but it slipped my mind with all the excitement in the last few days. It turns out Lukas can be very distracting...

My heart leaps when I see him pull up outside at six. Luckily, there's no one in the shop, so I don't have to shoo anyone out before grabbing my bag and locking up. Cujo is waiting in the back seat, but there's nothing on earth that can tear my eyes away from Lukas leaning against the side of the truck. I swear to God, my heart tries to jump out of my throat every time I see him.

He's traded his plain t-shirt for a soft black henley. He's pushed the sleeves up so his tattooed forearms are on display. He's so freaking sexy that I'm pretty sure he could give Jason Momoa a run for his money in that shirt. He runs his hand through this hair when he sees me, smiling smugly. "Like what you see, Freckles?"

I shrug noncommittally. "You look ok, I guess."

He rubs his beard with one hand, pinching the front of my dress and pulling me into him, careful not to bump my hand.

"Just ok? I guess I should try harder next time," he smirks at me like he can hear my heart thumping wildly in my chest. Then again, maybe he can. He seems to get everything about me. It doesn't even feel like a stretch that he'd know the second my heart starts to race for him.

"Happy Birthday, Freckles," he says before tilting his head and sealing his lips over mine. He helps me into the truck, insisting on buckling my seatbelt for me.

"I can do it," I argue.

"Yeah, but I like taking care of you, so let me."

I roll my eyes but let him help.

The drive to his grandmother's house is quick. Cars are lined up around the block, not surprising given the size of his family. I follow him to the door, filled with trepidation. I've spent plenty of time with his family, but it's always been as a friend of the girls. I hope it isn't too weird for them to see me with him. I'm not too worried about Olive and Julia, but I don't know what I'll do if Lilah can't come around.

The house is quiet when Lukas opens the front door, and I follow him inside. He takes Cujo's leash, looking around. The house is empty except for the smoky smell of grilling food.

"Huh… maybe they're all out back…" Lukas says, taking my hand and leading me through the house. He opens a door, holding it for me and gesturing for me to go ahead. Stepping out into the evening light, I freeze. The backyard is *filled* with people. White streamers and lanterns hang from the oak trees. A giant banner floats between the trees reading: "Happy Birthday Parker."

Olive, Julia, and Lilah are front and center, glasses raised as they lead a cheer of "Surprise!"

I drop Cujo's leash, overwhelmed, and cover my face with my good hand as I burst into tears.

Lukas wraps an arm around my shoulders and leans down. "Are you ok? I'm so sorry. I shouldn't have surprised you—"

"No!" I sob. "This is amazing. I just—I've never had a birthday party before," I say, looking back out at his sisters. All three are staring at me, frozen and wide-eyed. I wipe the tears from my eyes, willing them to stop as I laugh and apologize.

"I'm sorry. This is just… overwhelming."

Julia steps up, pulling me into her arms for a gentle hug. "Don't apologize!"

I swipe at the tears again. "I'm not great with surprises."

Lilah laughs and digs a pack of tissues out of her purse. "We should have known better. You happy-cry about everything."

"It's true," I say, laughing as I dab the last of the tears from my face. "This is really nice, you guys!"

"It was all Lukas," Lilah stage-whispers, holding a hand to her mouth conspiratorially.

I turn to glance back at him. He's smiling softly and mouths, "I love you."

It is by far the best birthday I've ever had. Lukas helps Asher grill a mountain of hamburgers, watching as his sisters drag me around to socialize. As promised, Gran fusses over my injured hand, alternately scolding me for putting myself in danger and telling me how proud she is of me for standing up for Cujo.

After dinner Olive brings out an enormous strawberry and cream cake and I blush about a dozen shades of red while everyone sings to me. Ben, Brooks and Asher build a fire in the big brick fire pit, arguing about the placement of each piece of wood, while Lilah and Olive look on, calling out suggestions and generally stirring up more trouble.

They all settle down once the fire is blazing. Brooks pulls Olive into his lap and whispers something in her ear that makes her eyebrows climb mischievously. I probably don't want to know, but it's still adorable.

Lilah stands up and clears her throat. Ben grins, standing behind her, arms wrapped protectively around her shoulders.

"Since we're all here, Ben and I have an announcement," she says loudly. Everyone shuts up so fast it's comical. "I'm pregnant," she says with a smile.

"We know!" Olive and Julia yell in unison.

Lilah gives them a quelling look before continuing. "And we're having twins," she says before sticking her tongue out at her sisters.

Olive screeches like a barn owl, and Julia cackles.

"Oh my God! Oh my God!" Olive jumps up and down while their

grandmother hustles to give Lilah a hug. She swats at Julia's shoulder as she passes, but Julia keeps laughing.

Lukas kisses his sister on the cheek and congratulates Ben while I give Lilah a one-armed hug.

"I knew you weren't drinking seltzer for fun," I tease her.

"I know," she laughs. "I just wanted to hit twelve weeks and make sure everything was ok before we broke the news. Thanks for being cool about it, unlike some people!" She raises her voice at Olive as she finishes her sentence but grins at her sister, still bouncing excitedly.

"How was I supposed to know? I just thought you were being sneaky for no reason! You could have dropped a hint, you know!"

Lukas and I settle on one of the log benches, watching the fire and listening to his family give Lilah a hard time. Cujo has been the life of the party, chasing every stick and wolfing down every bite of food that gets snuck his way, but he seems to have worn himself out. He sits next to me, his broad head resting on my thigh. Lukas kisses my temple, running his fingers up and down my arm.

"I love your family," I tell him.

"And they love you. Almost as much as I do," he replies. I fiddle with Cujo's collar, fingering the quality leather and big chunky buckle. I spin it to admire his shiny new tag, blinking to make sure I'm not seeing things. But I'm not imagining it, I realize, my heart pounding so hard I'm briefly worried I might have a heart attack.

Freshly engraved in the metal are the words:

Will you marry me?
Love, Lukas

Lukas is perfectly still, his hand unmoving on my arm. When I whip my head up to look at him, he's smiling but visibly nervous.

"Are you serious?" I ask quietly. He nods, leaning down to whisper in my ear.

"I know better than anyone that you don't need someone to take care of you, but I want to do it anyway. I want to be part of your adventure and your partner in crime. I love you and I can't live without you, Freckles. I want you to be my wife if you'll have me."

175

I pull back, searching his face. I almost can't believe this is real.

"Yes. Oh my God, yes." My voice climbs as I answer. I put a hand on his cheek, looking into his eyes. "I love you so much. Yes!"

"Oh, thank God," he exhales roughly. "Jesus, you scared me for a second," he laughs, taking a relieved breath. He reaches into his pocket, pulling out a box, and I can't help it when the tears well up in my eyes. He opens the box and pulls out a ring, the stone glittering in the firelight. He slips it on my finger and laughs sweetly, wiping the tears from my cheek.

"Don't cry," he whispers.

"I can't help it," I laugh, blinking the moisture away.

He cups my face, kissing me deeply.

"Hold the fuck up!" Olive yells from across the fire. "Did you just ask Parker to marry you?!"

The whole yard goes silent as they look from Olive to me and Lukas. I hold up my left hand so they can see the ring, turning back to Lukas. My body lights up as he buries his hands in my hair, kissing me as the cheers go up around us. He's the best man I've ever known. Neither of us is perfect, but we're more than perfect for each other.

EPILOGUE: PARKER

I watch in slow motion as Lilah passes me a glass of champagne, a flute of seltzer in her other hand, and her adorable pregnant belly filling out her party dress.

Oh shit.

Maybe my eyes give something away because she squints at me as I take the champagne, trying not to hold it like it could turn into a spider at any moment. I force a smile, trying to look like I'm not freaking out on the inside. For the record, I'm full-blown, screaming crazy, bouncing off the walls of my mind. But on the surface, I'm just a duck, floating on a pond, calm as can be.

My best friend's rehearsal dinner might be one of the single worst times to realize my period is late, but that actually says more about how amazing my life is than anything else. My shop has blown up into one of the top romance-only bookstores on the West Coast and a must-see tourist stop for anyone that loves romance.

The Mackenna Jade book signing turned out to be a turning point for Sorry, I'm Booked. Once I hosted her, I had authors requesting to do book signings so often that I had to hire someone to organize and run the events. I've been featured in travel magazines, blogs, and was even asked to do a spot on a national morning talk show.

And as amazing as all of that is, that's just work. Lukas is my life and I'm his. We can't get enough of each other. Even after hiring full-time help at the bookstore, the days I take off aren't enough time with him. There are mornings I wake up and can't believe how much my life has changed in four months. And now it might all change again...

Lukas is grinning at me from across the party, his dark hair and wide shoulders making his suit look like straight sin. He lifts his glass to me, winking, and I nearly swoon. I hope the way he affects me never wears off. I'm not sure how much of a bad boy he'll be at eighty-five, but I'll still love the hell out of him. Unbidden, the image of an aging Lukas peeling out on a Rascal flits through my head and I have to stifle a laugh.

Lilah taps the microphone set up on her patio, looking down the line at Julia, Chelsea, Sally, and me before giving her Maid of Honor toast. I smile like I'm paying attention, laughing when everyone else does, but all I can think of is when I can get out of here and find a pregnancy test. I do wonder how Lukas will react, though I'm not overly worried. He's got a soft spot for babies and we talked about having kids in the future. This would just be earlier than we planned.

Everyone raises their glasses and I toast along with them, putting the glass to my lips without drinking a drop. As soon as the party resumes, I set my glass on the catering tray, picking up a glass of water. One of Brooks' cousins restores classic cars, and he's been monopolizing my fiancé all night. I'm debating whether I should steal my man away or let him talk shop a little longer when I feel a hand tug on my elbow.

Lilah's eyes are knowing as she hooks her elbow with mine. "I saw that you know," she whispers conspiratorially.

"Saw what?" I ask with as much innocence as I can muster.

"You didn't drink the champagne, but you pretended to. You're pregnant, aren't you?" She's bouncing with excitement, green eyes sparkling.

"I don't know..." I whisper. "Maybe... I just realized I'm late. I might sneak off if that's ok? I don't know if I can stay here all night wondering."

"Oh, my God! This is awesome," she whispers before smiling at a guest I don't recognize and raising her voice. "Hi Susan! I'm so glad you could make it! Did you get one of the crab cakes?" She gently steers the woman the other way, tugging me towards the back door of her house and whispering, "Come on, I have a leftover pregnancy test upstairs."

Oh, thank God. I just need to know one way or the other.

I follow her up to her master bathroom, heart-pounding and grateful we don't run into any other party guests.

She digs around in the drawers of her vanity until she pulls out a blue box, holding it up triumphantly. "Ha! I knew I had one leftover! Here," she says, unwrapping the little stick. "Go pee on it!"

I stare at it, blood pounding in my ears. Why is that little thing so scary?!

"Maybe I should wait…"

"Hell no! You can't walk around worrying about this all night. And what are you going to do tomorrow? Pass off champagne and cocktails all night? Olive has more alcohol for this wedding than an entire naval fleet could drink in a week."

"I know," I groan. "Ok. Fine." I snatch the stick out of her hand and push her out of the bathroom. She laughs as I shut the door.

"I could have turned my back, you know," she laughs, her voice is muffled as I shut the door.

"Hell no!" I sit and hold the stick so I can pee on it. "This is gross!" I yell at her.

"*Pfft*," she scoffs. "It's just the first of the many indignities you'll get to enjoy with pregnancy. Wait until you see how enormous maternity panties are!" She cackles.

"Could you try not to sound so gleeful when you say that?" I ask. "Ok, I did it. Now what?"

"Put the cap on, set it down, and walk away!"

"What? Why?" I ask, alarmed. "How long does it take?" I'm trying not to look at it but it's flipping torture.

"A couple minutes."

I set a pile of clean toilet paper on the counter and lay the stick on top, but as I do, it's impossible to miss the big bold word in the window. Pregnant.

Pregnant.

Oh shit. Shit. Shit. Shit.

"Parker?" I hear Lilah's voice, but it sounds like I'm underwater. I can't focus on her right now. "Parker are you ok?" I sink to the floor and put my head between my knees, trying to control my breathing but I'm panicking, every breath sticking in my chest.

Lilah throws the door open and I'm vaguely aware of her rubbing my back.

"Hang on. Ok?" Lilah disappears and I'm just beginning to get my shit together when she reappears with Lukas hot on her heels.

He crosses the bathroom to me and the look on his face is every bit as panicky as I feel. His eyebrows shoot up when he sees the test on the counter, but he passes it by to sit next to me on the floor, pulling me into his lap. Lilah makes herself scarce, leaving Lukas to take care of me.

"You ok, Freckles," he asks, stroking my hair.

"I'm pregnant!" I blurt out.

He chuckles. "And you're not happy about it?"

"No, I am! I'm just…" It's hard to put the panic into words, but the gravity of bringing a baby into the world is just… so much pressure. The responsibility of it is overwhelming, and it's not like I had a great role model to go off of. "What if I'm a terrible mom?" I say, voice cracking.

Lukas laughs, loud and warm as he holds me tighter, tucking my head under his chin. "That's the craziest thing I've ever fucking heard. You know that, right? I've seen you punch someone for threatening to hurt an animal. You brought a hospital to its knees in defense of me. You love with your whole heart and body and soul. Our baby couldn't ask for a better mother."

Oh God. He always knows exactly what to say when it counts most. "God dammit, you're making me cry," I laugh through watery eyes.

"Better than panicking about crazy things," he jokes back. "Let's go. I'm taking you home."

"The party isn't over yet," I argue half-heartedly, looking up at him. Not for the first time tonight, I'm itching to unbutton his white dress

shirt and let him do dirty things to me with that necktie. I am dying
to get out of here, but I don't want to ditch my bridesmaid duties.

Lukas laughs. "Olive and Brooks took off already. He carried her
out over his shoulder." He shudders dramatically. "I'm assuming they
have a game of Parcheesi to finish."

"I mean they're about to get married, so I imagine they're going
to— "

Lukas claps a hand over my mouth. "Parcheesi."

I grin against his fingers. "Does that mean we can go home and
play Parcheesi?" I ask, my voice muffled as I bat my eyelashes at him.

"Fuck that," his voice drops as he strokes his fingertips down the
side of my throat. "I'm going to take the mother of my baby home and
fuck her so hard I knock her up again."

EPILOGUE: LUKAS

"**G**ive daddy a hug, Sophie."

I catch my daughter as she runs toward me, lifting her into the air. She wraps her arms around my neck and squeezes so hard I can barely breathe. She puts her warm hands on my cheeks and gives me a sloppy kiss before wriggling away.

"Lemme go daddy! Aunty Owive promised me candy!"

I give my sister a death glare over my toddler's head.

"She's all yours for the night, so on your own head be it," I tell Olive. "And don't tell Parker that you're sugaring her up."

Olive pushes me towards my truck with a sarcastic sigh. "Can you leave already? I have a favorite niece to spoil."

"Yay! Spoil me!" Sophie jumps up and down next to my sister, yanking on her hand. Her dark curls bounce around her bright blue eyes. She looks so much like my sisters, but those eyes and the light dusting of freckles on her nose are all Parker.

"Love you, baby," I say, wiggling my fingers at her. She blows me a kiss before turning and pulling Olive back towards the house, already rambling about all the things she wants to do. Olive and Brooks are the perfect babysitters; so fun that Sophie thinks she's getting away with everything and so terrified of something happening to her that I

182

know they won't let her out of their sight for even a second. Plus, Cujo is already inside, probably making himself comfortable on Olive's white sofa, and he's Sophie's personal guard dog.

I get to the bookshop five minutes before closing and lean against the side of my truck, just out of sight, waiting for my wife to finish up with her customers. When she locks up and starts down the street toward her car, I whistle to get her attention. She looks up, confused, but the smile that spreads across her face when she sees me is enough to light up even the blackest heart.

"Where you headed, Freckles? You wanna go for a ride?" She drops her phone in her bag as she saunters towards me. The last five years haven't changed the core of Parker, but the strength she used to hide has worked its way to the surface, making her more confident and beautiful every single day.

"I don't know," she says, looking me up and down coyly. "You look like trouble…" As soon as she's close enough, I hook a finger under the waistband of her skirt and pull her into me.

"I'm definitely trouble." Pulling her hair to the side, I kiss her neck, loving the way I can still make her shiver. "But you always did like a bad boy, didn't you?"

"Mm-hm," she sighs happily.

"I dropped Cujo and Sophie off with Olive, so I've got the whole night to do *really* bad things to you." I bite the sensitive spot where her shoulder and neck meet, making her breath hitch, a little moan climbing her throat. "Get your sexy ass in the truck, I'm kidnapping you," I say, giving her a quick kiss and opening the passenger door for her. I give her ass a smack as she climbs in, just for good measure.

We drive west with the windows down, parking at the trailhead for Kehoe with plenty of daylight left to enjoy the walk out to the beach. The sun glints low off the water as we crest the dunes to the beach and Parker grins, grabbing my bicep as she slips her shoes off. As soon as she's free, she runs to the water, shrieking when the cold surf hits her feet.

I'm prepared these days. A side effect of fatherhood, I guess. I pull the blanket out of my backpack and spread it out, anchoring it with some rocks before pulling out the bottle of wine I brought.

"God, you're the best," Parker says as she walks back up the beach. The sun dances through her coppery hair as the wind lashes it around her face and blows her skirt up her thighs.

"I aim to please." I grin at her as I pull the cork out of the bottle of wine. Parker laughs as I pull her down to sit between my legs and wrap my arms around her, taking a long pull from the bottle before passing it to her. She takes it, leaning her head back against my shoulder as she takes a sip. We sit and watch the waves, enjoying the rare, quiet moment of solitude.

Brushing her hair to the other side, I lean down and kiss her shoulder, nipping at the soft skin. Parker's breath hitches when I give her hair a gentle tug. She tilts her face, giving me better access. Running my nose up her neck, I breathe her in. The soft, familiar, peachy scent of her skin endlessly enticing.

Glancing around, I double-check that we're still alone on the beach. It would be a damn shame if I had to get up and chase anyone off right now. Luckily, it's deserted, the benefit of a beach you have to hike out to.

Slipping my hand under her shirt, I pull the lace of her bra down to free a breast. She moans when I roll her nipple between my fingers; her back arching against my chest. Parker squirms in front of me, grinding her ass against my hardening cock, gasping softly when I give the tight peak a hard pinch.

"You're sexy as fuck, Freckles," I whisper in her ear. "How wet is that little pussy?"

"I don't know. Maybe you should see for yourself," she whispers back.

Sliding my free hand under her knee, I lift it and put her leg over mine before drawing my knee up, spreading her wide. She trembles excitedly as I trail my fingers up her inner thigh and across the panel of her panties.

"Fucking hell," I groan. "You're soaked for me, Parker." Teasing my finger under the edge of her panties, I ease one finger into her pussy. She's hot, tight, and completely drenched. She gasps as I press a second finger inside her, stroking deep as I pull her leg wider and higher with mine. "Good girl. Spread those pretty legs for me," I growl in her ear. Parker shivers and her pussy squeezes my fingers.

I ease my fingers in and out, slowly but with a firm purpose as I grind the heel of my hand against her clit. She's panting and moaning in my lap, mewling like a kitten as I work her pussy, taking my time.

"You going to come on my hand?" I ask, knowing full well how close she is. Her legs tremble against mine, hips rocking desperately.

"Yes," she gasps, her hands gripping my thighs, fingertips digging into the muscle.

"Do it," I demand. "Come for me so I can put you on my lap and fuck this wet pussy like you deserve." My voice is hoarse. I need to get inside her so goddamn bad I'm shaking with it.

Parker's body tightens like a bowstring, body trembling as she comes. I clamp a hand over her mouth. She's a screamer and I know she can't help it. I don't think anyone is near enough to hear, but I sure as hell don't want someone coming to investigate.

As soon as her breathing catches up, I shift her forward, making room to unzip my pants. Parker turns on her hands and knees, the wind blowing her curls away from her face. She watches me, eyes full of lust as I free my aching cock. Sitting cross-legged, I pull her into my lap, straddling me. I yank her panties to the side, pulling her hips down, impaling her on my cock.

She throws her head back, crying out in pleasure. She's so tight; the pressure is overwhelming. "Fuck, that's good," I mutter into her neck, burying a hand in her hair and holding her tight.

"So good," she whispers, rocking against me.

I find Parker's lips with mine, kissing her hard. "Jesus Christ, baby." Gripping her hip with one hand, I help her grind down harder, swallowing her panting gasp. My cock swells impossibly hard, filling every inch of her wet pussy. Parker's fingers dig into my shoulders, twitching as she gets closer and closer. Sliding my fingers around the column of her throat, I hold her close, pressing my forehead to hers. Her lips part and I watch her gorgeous blue eyes flutter as she's swept up in pleasure, taking me with her.

We lay on the blanket for a long time, letting the sun set over the water while Parker lies on my chest. I slip my hand under the back of her shirt, stroking her soft skin. She and Sophie are my entire world. I have Parker to thank for everything. She's the architect of my happiness, the mother of my child, and my reason for living. I don't know what I did to deserve her, but she is my best adventure and I'll never let her go.

Parker looks up at me, a huge smile lighting up her face. "I'm hungry. You want tacos?"

"Christ, you're perfect," I laugh. "Yeah. Let's go, Freckles. Kidnapper pays."

FROM THE AUTHOR

Thank you so much for reading *Revved Up*! Every time I finish writing a book I think, "I can't possibly love another couple as much as I love this one." Parker and Lukas are no different. I loved writing their book. I loved letting Parker get dirtier and dirtier as the story went on, and I loved letting them discover each other. Every character feels real to me, but something about these two just made my heart sing.

I also LOVED Cujo. I grew up with a Rottweiler named Jess, who was the kindest, sweetest soul to ever walk the face of this earth. She was also so physically intimidating that she made grown men cross the street to avoid us. She defended and loved us unfailingly. She believed she was a lap dog and if you sat on the ground, she'd be on top of you, crushing your legs with her love. It's a beautiful thing to be an author and put pieces of yourself in a story. It makes my heart happy to immortalize Jess in writing Cujo.

I'm sure by now you've guessed that Julia is up next. I'm not going to lie; I have been dying to get to Julia ever since introducing her in *Stripped Down*. She's one of my favorite characters to write and seems to just fly out of my fingertips. Filled with banter and extra dirty, *Pent Up* is coming spring of 2021! Keep reading for an excerpt from Julia's book.

Also, if you loved *Revved Up* (or any of my books!) please leave a review on Amazon! Every review helps me out as an author. They don't need to be long or detailed. Just a quick, "Loved it" makes a huge difference. I read them all and I promise you, nothing makes an author happier than a kind review!

Thank you so much for your support.

--Mae

ACKNOWLEDGMENTS

As always, I feel like I have a million people to thank for helping me get this book into your hands. The act of writing is a solitary one but turning my rough manuscript into an actual book requires a lot of support, both professional and emotional.

To my loving husband and amazing children: Thank you for respecting the noise-cancelling headphones! My husband is an incredible man and the world's best father. I seriously don't know how I got so lucky, but I'm grateful for him every single day.

To my friend, editor, and confidant, Amy Maranville of Kraken Communications: I could kiss the ground you walk on. Whenever I'm having a bad day, need advice, or a safe person to vent to, I know I can reach out to you and you'll get me back on track. Thank you for encouraging me, pushing me, and on occasion, giving me the brutal honesty I need!

A huge hug and thank you to my beta readers and friends, Celia K. Nott, C.R. Riley, and April Claudina. You are the first line of defense when it comes to my books. I am so grateful for your thoughtful (and often hilarious) comments and guidance. My books wouldn't be the same without you.

To my author friends, Avery Maxwell, Claire Hastings, Juniper

Kerry, C.R. Riley, Celia K. Nott, and Mica Rae: I fucking love you. Your talent and genius are motivating as hell.

To Jules Malone of The Southern Belle's Bookshelf Editing and Consulting, the passionate and talented proofreader who polished every last inch of this novel. I can't even tell you what a relief it is to hand you my book baby and know that it's in loving hands.

And to my girlfriends Becky, Brittany, Emily, and Stacey. The four of you keep me sane. I don't know how I ever functioned without your friendship. I love you!

AN EXCERPT FROM PENT UP BY MAE HARDEN

Julia

I watch my brother-in-law spin Olive on the dance floor, her ivory skirt floating out around her like a fairy princess. There was a time when I thought none of us would get married, but here we are. Candles, flowers, plentiful cocktails, all we're missing is a drunken rendition of the chicken dance and we can call it a night.

Lilah's canoodling with Ben in a corner, looking like the fucking goddess of fertility. Parker and Lukas snuck off halfway thought the cocktail hour. I expect they'll turn up any minute, disheveled and half of the buttons ripped off their clothes. I swear to god, the two of them are single-handedly keeping the safety pin market afloat. And really, good for them. I can enjoy the fact that they've all found their people.

It's a nice thought; that there's someone out there for everyone. That Prince Charming is out there, waiting for me. The cold reality is that Prince Charming turned out to be a work obsessed douche bag and most of the guys I've dated would turn on a dime if someone offered them a quick blowjob. I am *so* much happier alone. I can rock the cool aunt vibe. Sally is single, and at sixty-five she's still making that shit look good.

For what it's worth, dating is just about the last thing on my mind these days. Long hours at the hospital have sucked every drop of energy from my body, and besides the annoyance of my onetime crush schmoozing his way through my sister's wedding, I have bigger problems at hand. I've been clutching my little purse all night, dreading the call that I know has to be coming.

Was I aware that the hospital's whistle-blower protection policy was a load of crap when I submitted the complaint? Hell no. But it doesn't change the fact that Doctor Grimaldi is a sack of human garbage. Even if my name gets out as the one who reported him, I can't find it in me to regret what I did. The whole point of becoming a nurse was to help people. I'm not about to stand aside and let an alcoholic get away with putting anyone in danger, especially children.

The music changes and the crowd claps as Brooks gives Olive one last spin and a dip. I consciously brighten my smile as I clap along. The wedding planner is eyeing me, and as tough as I am, she is absolutely terrifying. I'd sooner shave my head than get on her bad side.

The catering staff serves dinner with the robotic efficiency of a well-oiled machine, then there are toasts, and the cake cutting. I'm doing well, hiding the stress that's tearing me up inside. This is Olive's day and the last thing on this god forsaken earth I would ever do is let my personal shit get in the way.

Nope.

Today is all sunshine and rainbows. I can make it through this without batting an eyelash. Although… a drink definitely wouldn't hurt. It has been a long, long day and the servers aren't bringing wine around to the tables anymore.

"Want something from the bar?" I ask Asher.

"Nah," he grunts, holding up his beer.

"'Kay. Thanks for the chat," I say sarcastically, patting him on the back. He's never been much of a talker, but he seems to have reached all new levels of sullen lately.

Sally spots me on my way to the bar, hooking an arm through mine and whistling as she looks me up and down.

"God damn you make stretch velvet look good, girly."

"Well, I've got you to thank," I laugh. "You dressed me."

192

Sally hoots and leans back to look at my butt. "I might have picked the dress, but you're filling it out. Sweet Jesus. If you don't find a man tonight..." she sighs.

"You're the worst, you know that?" I tease, hugging her hard.

The bartender gives us a nod, and Sally asks him for two shots of tequila.

"Hard no! I'll take a glass of champagne."

"You're no fun," Sally pouts as the bartender pours me a glass, sliding it towards me. As I take it, my bag vibrates in my hand. Opening the clasp and peeking inside, I see Brenda's name on the screen. Fuuuck. She's my inside girl with the hospital administration. I'm thankful as hell that I brought her cupcakes from Olive's bakery for her birthday.

"Oh, I'm fun, but I'm not getting hammered with you at Olive's wedding. I've got to take this call. Go find Anita and Josie. They can keep up with you, at least."

Sally throws her drink back and scans the party. "Alright, fine. I'll see you later."

Abandoning my champagne and swerving through the crowd, I head for the edge of the tent as I answer.

"How bad is it?"

Brenda's nasally voice comes through, so quiet I can barely hear her. "Well, it's not great. Could be worse, though."

"Are you hiding in a supply closet? I can barely hear you." I try covering my other ear and ducking behind the catering tent to block out some of the party noise.

"Obviously. Where else could I call you from? I don't think I'm exactly supposed to be sharing this with you," she whispers back.

"Sorry, thanks for calling. This has been eating at me all day."

"I can imagine. They're going to put you on paid leave until-"

"What?" I screech at the phone, blood pounding in my ears. I wish there was a better word for how I sound, but "strangled eagle" is probably even less flattering.

"Look, it's short term. The facts and evidence are on your side, but Grimaldi is out for blood. He's trying to make it look like this is a personal vendetta."

"What the actual hell. I included video evidence of him drunk on hospital property. What more do they fucking need, Brenda?"

"Just time, Julia. I know that's hard to hear, but they have to get lawyers up to speed and protect the hospital. They've already put Grimaldi on unpaid leave while they investigate. They're going to ask you to come in and give the lawyers a deposition, but I wanted you to have a head start. The hospital isn't working against you, they're just covering their own asses. Still, couldn't hurt to get a lawyer, ok?"

"Yeah. Ok. Thank you."

"Anytime, hun."

She hangs up and I'm left standing alone behind a catering tent wondering what the fuck I do now. Lawyer up, I guess? I spent years studying and working my ass off to get where I am. I fought, scrambled, and clawed to get my position in the pediatric wing at the hospital and now it's all going to crash down around me. Administrative leave is a stain you can't wash off, no matter the reason they put you on it.

Weaving back to the bar, I eye my glass of champagne before sliding it back to the bartender.

"I changed my mind. Can I have that shot of tequila please?"

He grins at me with a slightly lecherous expression on his face as he pours a shot, spilling it over the side of the glass. He slides it toward me, along with a lime wedge on a napkin.

Ignoring the way he's watching me, I toss back the shot and bite into the lime.

"Rough night?" He asks.

"I'll take a fresh glass of champagne," I say, ignoring his question. If I wanted someone to talk about my problems with, it sure as hell wouldn't be this asshole.

"Hey Jules." A deep, smokey voice washes over me, sending a little tingle up my spine. *Hello.*

Turning, my eyes hit a wall of dress shirt and a black tie before climbing to the clean-shaven face of my childhood friend.

"Mateo!" I exclaim, throwing my arms around his neck and hugging him tight. He hugs me back, his arms wrapping around my back as he lifts me off my feet. "Lord, you've gotten big," I laugh as he sets me back down. He might be a year older than me, but we were matched for height when he enlisted in the Navy at eighteen.

His lips pull into the small, crooked smile I've known so long. He's always had a serious face. Stoic, even. But that brief smile is a dead giveaway that he's jumping up and down on the inside.

"I didn't think you were going to make it." I smack him on the chest lightly, just for keeping us in the dark.

"I couldn't miss Ollie's wedding."

"She'll stab you with her decorative cake knife if she hears you call her that," I warn him. "I missed you earlier."

His smile grows just a fraction. "I snuck in the back right before the ceremony. You were impossible to miss."

"It's hard to miss a bridesmaid. We get to stand up front and everything."

Mateo runs a thumb over his lower lip, distracting me for a split second before my eyes meet his again. I'm not one for the clean shaven, uptight look but I have to admit, he's really grown into it.

"Is everything ok, Jules?"

I look up at him sharply. "Of course, why?"

He gives his a head a casual little shake. "Just checking. I passed by the catering tent a couple minutes ago and you didn't seem thrilled about the phone call you were on, that's all."

I get the impression I'm not fooling him, but he's enough of a gentleman to let it go. "Just work shit."

"Uh-huh."

The bartender leans over the bar with a smarmy grin as he slides a glass of champagne toward me. "Can I get you anything else, sweetheart?"

I'm about to unleash all hell when Mateo takes my elbow, gently pulling me a step back as he slides between my body and the bar. His spine straightens, and he clenches his jaw as he stares the bartender down with an expression that I can only describe as "I'm gonna fuck you up in about three seconds."

The bartender looks terrified, backpedaling so hard I want to laugh. "I am so sorry, that came out wrong. Please let me know if I can help you with anything else, ma'am." He books it to the other end of the bar, avoiding looking in our direction.

"I could have handled that," I tell Mateo, smacking his bicep with the back of my hand. He turns to look at me, straight faced except for a tiny twitch at the corner of his lips.

"I know, Jules. I doubt there's anything on this earth you couldn't handle. But that was kind of fun." The twitch turns into a hint of a smile. I move to pick up the glass, but he slides it away. "I wouldn't drink anything he poured."

"You're right," I say as I reach over the bar, snagging an unopened bottle of champagne from a bucket of ice and two clean glasses. The bartender pretends he doesn't see me, unwilling to go toe to toe with Mateo. That's useful.

"That wasn't exactly what I meant." Mateo runs a thumb over his lower lip again, fighting to contain the smile that I know is trying to surface.

I bat my eyelashes as I pour a drink for each of us. "I know. You're a rule follower."

"How can you make that sound like a bad thing?" He asks with a soft chuckle.

"It's not. It's very admirable…"

"But?"

"But a rule follower wouldn't have a personal bottle of champagne." I grin as I hand him one glass and clink it with my own.

"True," he concedes. The tequila is softening the stress of Brenda's call and Stevie Wonder is crooning the opening lines of For Once In My Life. God, I love this song. Throwing back my glass of champagne, I tug on Mateo's elbow.

"Come dance," I demand. He resists but lets me tug him out to the middle of the tent.

"I'm a terrible dancer," he groans, chugging his glass and setting it on an abandoned table.

"No one cares," I laugh as he shuffles next to me, so stiff you'd think he was drinking just as much starch as he uses to iron his clothes. His dad waves at us from a table with my Gran before rubbing his elbow. "Is Luis ok?" I ask over the music.

"Yeah, he said he pulled something in his arm. Olive has him taking it easy at the bakery this week."

I nod but keep an eye on Luis, anyway. He looks worn down. Frankly, I think he needs to cut back or retire. I can't help worrying about him. He's the closest thing I have to an actual father.

The song ends and a new slower tempo starts up. I turn to head off the dance floor, but Mateo gently hooks a hand around my elbow.

"Oh, no you don't. This is the kind of dancing I can actually do," he says, pulling me back toward him. I glance up at his face, too surprised to argue as he takes my hand in his and slides the other around to the small of my back. I place a hand on his shoulder and let him sway me. The warmth of his hand seeps through the back of my dress, making my skin tingle. I don't think I ever noticed that he smells nice, but he does. Like cedar and a spice I can't place...

Holy shit. I definitely shouldn't be smelling my friend. I'm sure he's always smelled like that. It just didn't register because we haven't been this close since we were kids.

"You look so worried, Jules. Am I that bad of a dance partner?" His expression is still serious, but there's a glint of humor in his eyes. I usually go for the roguish men, often bordering on pirate levels of bad boy, but Jesus, I'm seeing the appeal of those Navy Seal romances Parker sells.

"No," I laugh breathlessly. "I just didn't peg you for a slow dancing kind of guy." A tipsy couple bumps into my back hard and I stumble into Mateo awkwardly. He pulls me closer, my breasts pressed against his chest as he steers me away from them, putting his body between me and the rowdies.

"You used to make me dance with you when we were little. Don't you remember?"

"Yeah, well, I was five. I thought I was going to be Cinderella."

Mateo laughs, a rare smile lifting his lips enough to show a hint of the dimple in his left cheek. The sound is rich and deep, vibrating through me like it was my own. "Cinderella has nothing on you, Jules."

"Why? Because I get to keep my dress on at midnight?"

Mateo's eyes flare as the song ends, his fingers flexing against my

197

back before he drops my hand and steps back. He clears his throat. "Probably for the best."

What the actual fuck? I pull back, stung. I may not be the blushing virgin, but I'm not ashamed of myself either. I'm sure he likes his girls sweet and innocent. I bet he likes them to fall in line and follow the rules too. That will *never* be me.

I laugh disbelievingly and shake my head. I don't know where the hell my head is at lately. "I'll see you around, Mateo."

I leave him in the middle of the dance floor and march to the bar, reaching over to take a fresh bottle of champagne. I point at the bartender as he opens his mouth to say something. "Don't fucking start with me," I threaten before stomping off to find Sally. My pool of drinking buddies may have shrunk because of pregnancy and wedding duties, but she's a sure bet.

ALSO BY MAE HARDEN

Stripped Down

Mowed Over

Revved Up

Pent Up - Spring 2021

Manufactured by Amazon.ca
Bolton, ON

17784828R00120